DEMONIC ANTHOLOGY VOLUME III
A Dark Humor Short Story Collection

I0584282

DEMONIC CARNIVAL
FIRST TICKET'S FREE

DEMONIC ANTHOLOGY VOLUME III
A Dark Humor Short Story Collection

DEMONIC CARNIVAL
FIRST TICKET'S FREE

Includes Stories By:

A. E. Santana	Angelique Fawns	Brandon Mead	Charlotte Platt
Chrissy Moon	Erika Lance	F.D. Gross	George Alan Bradley
Jeremy Rodden	Jessica Chaleff	K. Walker	Kerilyn Blake
Kerry Evelyn	Kim Plasket	Larry Griffin
M.B. Meraki	Ross Ellison	Stephen Herczeg
Teresa Edmond-Sargeant	Valerie Puri

4 Horsemen
Publications, Inc.

4 Horsemen Publications, Inc.
1497 Main St. Suite 169
Dunedin, FL 34698
4horsemenpublications.com
info@4horsemenpublications.com

Cover & Typesetting by Battle Goddess Productions

Paperback ISBN-13: 978-1-64450-641-7
Ebook ISBN-13: 978-1-64450-640-0

DEDICATION

To the Authors within and their families. Without you and your patience, there would be no collection to share with the world. May the rest of 2019 and the years to follow be fruitful for you all and here's to a wonderous journey.

Acknowledgements

I want to say thank you to everyone who continues to cheer me on. No amount of words could express how much you have kept my morale and spirit high in the lowest moments. Many of you remind me often that I can be the "Busiest Author in All of Orlando" and it means the world to me that my chaos shines through.

A special thank you to those who help make this anthology come together including my partner in crime Kim Plasket and my amazing review duo Ryan O'Reilly and Karen Webster. Without them, the anthology wouldn't get off the ground and they keep me moving forward, even if I'm the one holding things up!

Thank you to all the authors who submitted! This year I had to send quite a few rejections out and be picky. I hope you all have great success in the not-so-distant future.

And of course, the readers who gave support for the first volume, Demonic Wildlife and those who've continued to follow the Demonic Anthologies as we continue to grow.

Thank you to my husband, Justin, and the boys, Levi and Link, for being understanding and patient with Mommy's hard work and devotion.

To my writing villages here in Orlando, Florida which include Writer's Atelier and Racquel Henry, Anthony Awtrey & L.E. Perez with Orlando East Writers Group, and the misfit crew from Writers of Central Florida & Thereabouts.

READERS BEWARE

ou are traveling into a dark and humorous place. We start you off with light, soft stories, but be warned.

You will find yourself falling into the ever darker, gorier, and more demonic stories with each passing story. From heartwarming endings to feeling like you just walked out of the Carnival Port-a-potty into another dimension - this collection will leave your mind spinning.

The Fried Food stall, the Ferris Wheel, and even that carnival themed hotel in Vegas... all of it will never be the same for you after your visit to the Demonic Carnival. Remember... First Ticket's Free...

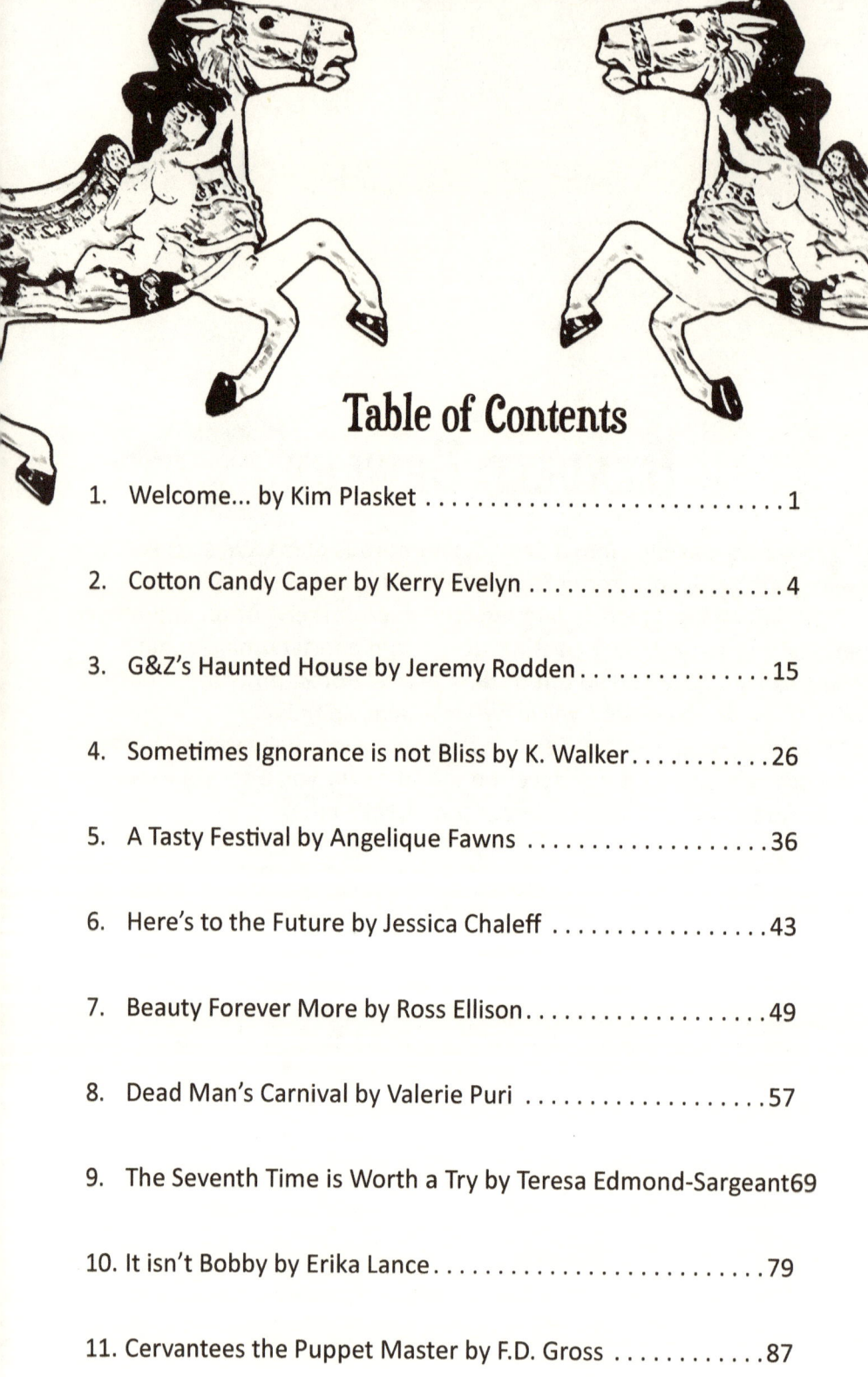

Table of Contents

WELCOME...

Kim Plasket

pproaching the small weather-beaten old ticket booth, you stop for a moment and look closely. The paint is garish and for some reason, it doesn't quite seem to fit, something about it makes you stop and pause. The huge fence behind the booth gives you no clue as to what may lay behind it. You figure you will just walk on by when the small door opens and a man appears.

"Come a little closer. Do you want to hear about the carnival?" His eyes were hypnotic if you could get past his greasy hair and the odor surrounding him of beer and elephant dung. "I have tales to tell you of the carnival. Listen to the screams; are those from joy or terror? Is that excitement of fear that you hear? They are simply people such as you enjoying what we have to offer."

You think to yourself he's the same as all the other salesmen, but something in the screams from behind the fence make you wonder, *is it pleasure or something darker, painful?* Maybe this is something new, something you haven't seen before? The last time you went to a carnival you were so young but remember the bright colors, flashing lights, and campy music that all failed to hide the truth only you could see.

The smiles on the carnies were fake; it was as if they were simply painted on. The men and women who manned the games and took care of the rides had eyes as black as night. You knew they were empty shells; they may not have been alive but still, they moved. You stand there for a

1

moment thinking, well aware of his eyes watching as if he can hear your thoughts.

He stares at you waiting for you to decide before he continues his tale, his sale. As you stare at the fence you swear you can smell blood, but the faint hint of peanuts and sawdust drown it out. Your skin begins to crawl as your mind fills with images of clowns hiding every corner. Fire-eaters ready to inflame you as you step through the gate; they take no prisoners. The lion tamers releasing their lions to attack if you dare to take any longer to make up your feeble mind.

You casually shake your head to dispel the images and his face falls as if you denied him a longed-for dream. Hurriedly, you tell him to please continue.

"My new friend, you will laugh with delight and scream with joy as our carnival works its magic into your very soul. I promise you, you may never leave."

You feel drawn closer to him. It's hard to believe you thought the odor emanating off of him was disgusting, wondering how you could've been so mistaken. He smells delightful, his eyes promising you joys beyond your imagination.

You find yourself asking him "How much for a ticket?"

His eyes begin to glow with fire as the gates behind him slowly open, Arms wide he declares:

"The first ticket's free."

About the Author

Kim Plasket is a Jersey girl at heart relocated to sunny Florida. She enjoys writing mainly horror and paranormal stories and lives with her husband and 2 kids. When she is not slaving away at her day job, she can be found drinking coffee with fellow author Valerie Willis and planning the demise of some poor character. Currently, she has several short stories featured in anthologies such as 'Demonic Wildlife' and 'The Hunted', also has a story in an Anthology Titled Fireflies and Fairy dust she also has had a story featured in Shades of Santa. Also the newly released DrabbleDark Anthology, Work of hearts magazine. She has stories in Trembling With Fear, more tales from the tree. Just released. Thrill of the Hunt: Buried Alive. Coming out later this year Demonic Carnival: First Ticket's free.

She also has several short stories and a post for Women in Horror Month on the website The Horror Tree.

https://www.amazon.com/-/e/B074YCLRCF

Cotton Candy Caper

Kerry Evelyn

The enemy's trace was in the air. His thick and unmistakable scent of fear and anger penetrated Sammi's pores and mingled with the excitement from a crowd.

She caught sight of him up ahead as he turned onto the cliffside road. *He's heading for the church carnival!* She should have guessed this was where he would strike.

He was clever—she'd give him that. But Sammi had an edge over him that he never counted on. She'd used it before—and she'd use it again.

She scanned the church grounds. The fall carnival bustled with activity. To her right, food trucks and snack booths backed up to the road. Straight in front of her, traditional games were scattered among local artists, crafters, and vendors. The rides were further back, set against a crop of trees that marked the town line.

Sammi lost the scent behind the hand-washing station. *Where could he impart the most damage?* She swung her head toward the rides. A loose pin or computer malfunction could certainly harm the occupants.

She quickened her pace. She had to find him. Fast.

Sammi's ear twitched a few moments later. She picked up on a sibling quarrel nearby. She was getting close.

"This cotton candy tastes weird." A teenage girl frowned. "Has anyone seen Jordan yet?"

"Maybe he decided not to come 'cause you're a whiny baby." One of the elementary-age twin boys with her held his cotton candy out to an older woman. "I don't like it either. Can we get something else, Mom?"

"Shut up, Christopher," the teenage girl snapped. "You're the whiny baby."

"Not right now he isn't." Christopher's twin piped in. "I want a candy apple instead. This is gross."

"Mellie, Christopher, and Colton Walker, stop bickering! The only thing weird about your cotton candy is that it's full of sugar, and you're not used to that. You want a refund, go ask."

"Oh, Mom," Mellie groaned. She thrust the paper cone of cotton fluff at her mother. "You try."

Their mother pulled off a wisp of pink fuzz and sniffed it. "Smells like cotton candy to me." She took a bite. "Ech. You're right. That's awful."

Sammi watched as Mellie reluctantly led her brothers back to the cotton candy booth, where an elderly gentleman twirled the spun sugar onto white paper cones.

Her mother marched straight to the cotton candy vendor. "Who are you?" She stuck out her hand to the elderly man behind the machine. "Tracy Walker, chief carnival organizer. I've never seen you before. You're not on my volunteer list. Brett O'Hara is supposed to be here."

"I, um, I'm filling in." The man fixed his gaze on Tracy. "Brett had...a thing to do."

Tracy raised a brow. "Really? Because he promised me to my face he'd stick around all day and not chase after girls this year. Guess that lasted a hot second." She snorted. "So, who are you, then?"

"Malthace O'Malley. I was passing through your town today and spotted the carnival. I came right over. Brett was talking to a nice young lady, and I offered to help out for a bit."

Wolf in sheep's clothing, Sammi thought.

"How nice. Well, you're not mixing it right or something." Tracy slid through the space between the cotton candy booth and the candy apple booth next to it. He stepped to the side. "Let me see... Hmmm...everything looks right." She glanced at him. "Show me how you did it."

Malthace went through the motions of pouring in the sugar and spinning a perfect cloud of pink cotton. "See?" he said. "Perfect as this crisp autumn day by the sea."

Tracy held out a clump to each of her kids.

"Tastes fine," Mellie said.

"Better," Christopher agreed.

"I still want a candy apple," Colton insisted.

Tracy sighed.

Malthace smirked as the family walked away with their plain cotton candy. No one else he'd served seemed to notice the taste was off. Anytime now....

Ahh... There it was. The notes of the first argument drifted his way. His secret ingredient was working. Fifteen feet away at the Cliffside Diner's booth, owner Sadie Donovan held up one of her lemon pies, poised only inches from her husband Steve's face.

"I told you that lemon pie wouldn't sell! Apple, blueberry, pumpkin! That's what you buy at fall carnivals in Maine. Not lemon!" A telltale pink wisp clung to Steve's chin.

"You're insane, you know that?" The pie continued to hover threat-eningly. "The townies of Crane's Cove love *all* my pies, and they can get the other kind anywhere you go this time of year from Maine to Georgia! Forgive me if I dare to try something different!" With a huff, she marched off.

Excellent.

"I told you, I will *not* be your friend!" Malthace swung his head in the direction of an indignant small girl of about six standing with her arms crossed. In front of her, a preschool-aged boy stood, lower lip trembling.

"But you're my *sister*, Lydia!" the young boy wailed.

Malthace was almost giddy with excitement as he continued to hand out cotton candy to the young, old, and in between. It didn't matter how old you were, spun sugar was a treat that children loved and brought adults back to their childhood. He had been counting on that.

One particular adult, especially. As he waited patiently for his long-ago buddy, Malthace reflected on how close he was to getting his Reward. Decades ago, he'd made a bargain. It had both saved his life and killed his future. Now there was a way out, and he was taking it.

Ah, there he was now. A girl in her twenties pushed the man in a wheelchair right by the cotton candy booth. He'd recognize that face anywhere.

Turn around. You want the cotton candy.

She paused. "Did you want a snack, Uncle Charley?"

"I'd love one, Kat. Cotton candy?" the old man replied.

"You got it." She parked him off to the side and dropped a one-dollar bill in the donation jar.

"Here you go," Malthace said. *So young. So unsuspecting.*

"Thanks!"

He watched her bring it back to her uncle and smiled as he consumed the cone with impressive speed for an old man.

"Uncle Charley? Are you okay? You ate that really fast..."

Sammi observed the old man's pallor change in the seconds that followed his inhalation of the sugary treat. Charley groaned and clutched his abdomen.

"Kat? I don't feel—" His eyes closed, and he slumped in his chair. *Oh, no.* Dare she risk drawing attention to herself before she found who she was looking for?

It was time to move in. He was exhibiting signs of diabetic shock. Her years as a registered nurse still served her in her new role.

"Sir, are you okay?" She knelt in front of him and took his hand, feeling for a pulse. He moaned but didn't open his eyes. She turned to Kat, who face was twisted with grief. "Is he diabetic? Or epileptic?"

"He has a history of heart problems," she said as she pulled on her hair. I can't remember what exactly, but I can find Dr. Lightfeather. I saw him here—"

"It's okay," Sammi assured her.

"He was eating the cotton candy, and then he just started to look weird, and then—"

"Kat, I got him. Call 9-1-1."

"Right!" Kat fumbled with her phone as people gathered around.

Sammi stayed with the old man and grandniece until the paramedics arrived. After he was loaded onto the stretcher, she headed straight for the cotton candy booth.

DEMONIC CARNIVAL

It was time to go. He'd been found out. He'd done enough damage to pay his debt. The townspeople of this perfect little place were experiencing real life for once. What it felt like to be unloved, unwanted, unappreciated, and helpless. The pain was spreading. *Anytime now, Master. I'm ready.*

Charley Wetherby might even die. *A life for a life.*

Malthace slipped away from the booth and around to the backside of the church. He hadn't figured out an exit plan, but he didn't think he'd need one. But he was still here. Had he not completed the job to satisfaction?

Sammi's nose wrinkled. She was close.

She caught sight of the cotton candy vendor striding away from the booth. He disappeared around the back of the church. *The old man? It couldn't be.* But she knew it could. The devil was clever. It was just his way to send a harmless-looking grandfatherly type to do his dirty work. No one would expect it. Heck, *she* hadn't expected it the three times she'd walked past his booth.

"Stop right there!" Sammi commanded.

He froze. She held his gaze, the force behind it paralyzing him. "What did you put in the cotton candy?"

His hand relaxed its grip and a vial fell to the ground. She opened her palm and mentally summoned the vial to her. It zipped through the air between them and landed neatly in her outstretched hand. Sammi removed the cork and inhaled deeply. "Nicotine and nicene?" She stared the man in the eyes. "Tell me why."

"Why not?" Malthace shrugged. "It's addictive and affective. Added a little epinephrine for good measure. The people here are too perfect. Let them live life like the rest of the world."

"The people here choose to live life differently. They choose love. Do you remember what that feels like?"

"I try to forget." Malthace cocked his head as Sammi penetrated his mind to see his thoughts. A flash of a face, of a mother kissing him

8

goodnight as a small child. He grimaced. Another flash. Him on his knees, sliding a ring on to an outstretched fourth finger. He cried out, crippled by the pain as he collapsed forward. A third flash. This time he was bargaining for their lives.

"Love got me here," he spat, struggling to stand.

"No," Sammi said. "That wasn't love." She advanced a step closer and offered her hand. He glared at her, but eventually accepted it. She pulled him up.

The lines in his face twitched as he struggled to keep his composure. "I am bound in servitude until my debt is paid."

"If you'd truly chosen love, you'd have no debt." Sammi felt pity for the old man. "You saw Charley as a threat and made your deal to ensure she'd pick you. You didn't give her a choice to make that decision, and it's haunted you since."

"Love is a myth."

"I can prove to you it's not."

The old man shrugged. "Fine. Let's see you try. Doesn't look like I'm going anywhere, anyway."

Sammi held the vial up and spoke over it. Inside, the liquid swirled like a tiny tornado as the color changed from light mauve to a translucent pink. "This is no longer poison. This is a healing serum, an antidote, and love potion. It will restore the love in the hearts of all who consume it." She frowned. How would she get it to everyone?

"Come with me," she commanded. He followed her back to the food area. *The hand sanitizer!*

They arrived at the hand-washing station. She handed him the vial. "I'm going to wash my hands. The hand sanitizer dispenser is going to pop open and the bag of liquid is going to fall to the ground and burst. You'll offer to help. I'm assuming the refills will be in a box under the table. Twist open the bag and pour half the antidote in. We'll reset the dispenser. I noticed bottles of hand sanitizer are set out at some of the food booths. I'll grab two of them and we'll add the rest of the potion to those, then we'll walk around and offer squirts to anyone we see arguing. Any questions?"

He shook his head.

"Let's go."

Demonic Carnival

Ten minutes later, the dispenser was refilled. Malthace stood by the carousel holding a travel-sized pump bottle Sammi conjured. Malthace observed the crowd with skeptical cynicism. Sammi's plan couldn't possibly work—could it?

A teenage couple approached the line, the tension palpable between them. The girl stood with her arms crossed, lips pressed together. Behind her, the young man stammered as he clutched a stuffed unicorn.

"B-but Mellie, you told me you loved unicorns—"

"That was last week. Don't you pay any attention to me at all? I should have stayed with my little brothers. At least they listen to me half the time."

Here goes nothing. He approached the teens. "Excuse me, but didn't I see you earlier at the cotton candy booth? Can I offer you some hand sanitizer?"

"Whatever." She uncrossed her arms and held out her hands. He squirted a drop in each and looked up at the young man. He tucked the unicorn under an arm and opened up his palms.

He watched the transformation, fascinated. Within seconds, the muscles in their faces relaxed. Mellie's eyes widened and she flung her arms around her boyfriend. "I'm sorry, Jordan. I don't know what got into me. I love unicorns. Can you forgive me?"

A strange wave of *something* coursed through Malthace's body. His chest felt tight. His mouth twitched, as if it wanted to smile. He kept it in check.

Behind him, a little boy was crying. Next to him, a little girl was eating the cursed cotton candy, indifferent to his sobs and the gentle words his mother spoke to them.

"She doesn't *hate* you, Joey." Their mother shifted the baby she was carrying to her other arm, sunk down to Joey's level, and held out her free arm.

"Yes, she does! She *said* so!" Joey pressed himself against her and sobbed.

"She didn't mean it. You're the only brother she has. She loves you." She patted his back soothingly.

"She said she wished I wasn't born!"

Malthace shuffled over and squatted down next to the boy. "Hi, there."

The woman shot him a warning look. "Can I help you?"

"I might be able to help you," he said. He turned to the little girl who was polishing off the last of the pink sugar crystals that clung to the cone.

"I bet your hands are sticky. I'll trade that messy cone for a squirt of this to clean your hands, okay?"

She thrust her sugar-crusted palms at him. "Okay."

The little girl rubbed her hands together. "All clean." She turned to her brother. "Joey, I don't hate you. I'm sorry I didn't share my treat."

He continued to wander around and dispense the solution. He was feeling a bit dazed when Sammi found him. Was this how the Grinch felt when he gave Christmas back to the Whos?

"What do you think?" she asked.

"I feel...weird."

She grinned. "You feel love." She placed a hand on his shoulder. "You did good, Malthace."

He turned to her, troubled. "There's one more...Charley Wetherby. He went to the hospital."

"I'll get you there." Sammi eyed his almost-empty bottle. There should be enough left to get the job done. She put her hand on his shoulder and they faded into the soft summer breeze.

Sammi and Malthace reappeared on a bench outside the Emergency Department. It was a full hour's drive from the church to the hospital. If Charley Wetherby had been critical, the paramedics would have called for a medflight. It was good news he'd been taken in the ambulance, and they'd be ready when it arrived.

Any minute now.

"C'mon." Sammi led Malthace into the building. With the snap of her fingers, they were dressed in scrubs, complete with identity badges that could bypass security, if needed.

"How are we going to get it to him?" Malthace's eyes darted up and down the hallway.

"We'll fade out and follow him in. I've got an ounce of straight antidote for him. First chance you get, drop it into his mouth, under his tongue. It's the fastest way into the bloodstream."

The automatic doors opened and the team working on Charley Wetherby entered, shouting stats and directives. Sammi and Malthace faded into the air and followed them through the ED.

"Eighty-plus-year-old veteran diabetic with congenital heart disease, lost consciousness after eating cotton candy at a carnival. BP elevated but stable, oxygen is 96%.

A doctor and team of nurses crowded around the stretcher as it traveled toward an open room. "Transfer on my count... One...two...three!"

Sammi felt a nudge as Malthace slunk by her. She watched from the foot of the bed as Charley Wetherby's oxygen mask lifted ever so lightly. Invisible fingers pulled at his lips and the mask was set right again.

Charley Wetherby's icy cerulean eyes snapped open. He coughed, sputtered, and struggled to sit up.

Sammi reached out and grabbed Malthace's arm when she caught his now-familiar salty scent. She closed her eyes.

They reappeared outside the ED, sans scrubs. She sank down on the nearby bench. "You did it."

"He's going to be okay?"

"He is."

"What's going to happen to me now?" Malthace asked. He hung his head. "I failed to keep my end of the bargain."

"Love is more powerful than any bargain you made, Malthace."

"Really? After all I've done?"

"There is always forgiveness and redemption with repentance. Hold my hand."

A moment later, they were atop a rocky cliff, not far down from the church.

"What are we doing here?" Malthace asked.

"This is where you get your wings."

"I don't understand. What's happening?" He scrunched his face in confusion.

"You made a bargain with the devil, Malthace. You were consumed by anger, guilt, and revenge. You promised your soul for the love of the woman you loved. That's not the right way of things." Sammi's expression softened. "I know you loved her, and it's no one's fault that she died. But when you made the bargain to take her from Charley, you tainted your love for her. The doubt inside you grew and grew over decades as you wondered if her love for you was true or fabricated by the devil. You became so desperate to know, and when she died, you realized how you'd been tricked. The only way for you to stay alive after she died was if someone took your place. It's not Charley Wetherby's time. When you chose love instead, your fate changed. It's your time. Time to fly home to your love."

"Fly? What do you mean? Oh, my, I feel—" Malthace stumbled and reached out to Sammi. The heaviness of a lifetime of pain lifted from the wrinkles in his face. The dark circles under his eyes faded and his pupils transformed from dark green to a striking light blue.

Sammi held his forearms to steady him. Snowy white wings sprouted out of his back, and he began to glow.

His eyes widened in awe. "I can't believe it. A whole lifetime of bitterness, resentment, hate. I don't deserve this."

Sammi smiled. "You do. All that is erased. Go in peace, dear friend."

She watched him ascend, up, up, up. Another soul saved.

Today was a good day, indeed.

ABOUT THE AUTHOR

Kerry Evelyn is a native of the Massachusetts SouthCoast and now lives in Orlando. She loves God, her crazy family, books of all kinds, traveling, taking selfies, sweet drinks, and escaping into her imagination, where every child is happy and healthy, every house has a library, and her hubby wears coattails and a top hat 24/7. She is an educator, mentor, presenter, and the author of the Crane's Cove series, #sweetresortromance set in coastal Maine and a Guest Author for the Cat's Paw Cove series, set just south of St. Augustine, Florida.

You can find Kerry on Facebook @KerryEvelynAuthor, Instagram @KerryEvelynAuthor, and Twitter @theKerryEvelyn and follow her on Amazon and BookBub. Sign up for her newsletter and find more at KerryEvelyn.com and www.Facebook.com/groups/CranesCoveCrew.

G&Z's Haunted House

Jeremy Rodden

"**W**ell, what do you suppose this is all about, Z?" G asked his partner Z.

Z scratched his exposed brain in puzzlement. This would have been an odd situation if he weren't a zombie and part of his brain was exposed. It was still kind of weird, but at least being a zombie meant that he could scratch his exposed brain without causing any real damage. Z developed this as a bit of an unconscious habit since he and G first came into existence in Toonopolis.

"I have no idea," Z finally answered.

G floated closer to the hand-painted sign that declared "Free Haunted House This Way" with an arrow pointing at their home. Floating was the only way G could travel, being a ghost and all. He took off his horn-rimmed glasses and rubbed them on the white sheet-like material that made up his exterior. After replacing the glasses over the holes in the 'sheet', he read the sign again.

"So you didn't put this sign up?" Z asked.

"Obviously not. You?"

"Nope."

"Hrm," G puzzled. He looked over the sign at their house. While it wouldn't be a stretch to call it haunted, considering a ghost and a zombie lived there, it certainly wasn't free – or a tourist attraction in some kind of carnival. G's half of the house was full of gothic decorations such as tall spires and gargoyle statues, which was fitting because his half of the house was in the Gothicville section of the cartoon city.

"I second that 'hrm'," Z added, also looking up at their house. His half of the house was rundown and abandoned looking, also fitting since it was in the Dystopia Z section of Toonopolis – the one where zombie apocalypse related creations existed.

G trailed his gaze from the house and back to the sign that was definitely not there when they went for a walk. He inspected it more closely. "You smell that, Z?"

Z pointed to the gaping hole in his face where his nose used to be when he was alive. "I can't smell, G. And I've asked you to not be a jerk about that fact. I still don't know how you can smell." Z pointed to his partner, who was also seemingly sans-nose but he didn't really know what was under the sheet . . . or if anything was actually under there. The two of them never really figured that part out.

"I smell angst, shame, and marginally repressed insecurity," G explained.

"I may not have a nose, but none of those things are scents."

G shrugged. "Okay fine, I smell body odor unsuccessfully masked by a spray deodorant, which could only mean one thing?"

"Oh come on, not that guy again," Z lamented. "That Internet Troll has been trying to prank us ever since we got here and it's never gone well for him. And this one is lame." Z shambled to the haunted house sign presumably placed by the Internet Troll of Gothicville and reached out for it.

"Wait," G said, stopping Z from removing the sign. "I think we should see how this plays out. I have an idea." G smiled, or at least his eyes moved in such a way as to suggest he was smiling since he didn't have a mouth per se.

"Are you thinking what I'm thinking?" Z asked.

The ghost and zombie looked at each other and said simultaneously, "Home Alone." They high-fived then struck off to prepare for the impending invasion of their home.

The Internet Troll giggled to himself from his parents' basement in Gothicville. His plan to finally out-prank the ghost and zombie weirdoes that lived on the border of Gothicville and Dystopia Z was going to be great. They were going to be so annoyed when a bunch of tourists started walking into their house and thinking it was a tourist attraction.

"I'm so funny and clever," he thought to himself. He groaned as he stood from his computer chair and ran his fingers through his greasy hair. "This is gonna make those snowflakes rage so bad they'll need a safe space inside their safe space." He donned a hat that read 'World's Greatest Tour Guide' and made his way up the stairs with much respiratory effort.

"Goin' out mom. Be back later," he called into the kitchen.

His mother poked her head from the kitchen. She held a phone to her ear. "Hang on a second, Eugene."

"But mo-om," he whined, pronouncing 'mom' with two syllables for emphasis.

"Yes, I can help you with that," she said into the phone receiver. Hanging up the phone and untying her white apron, Eugene's mother addressed her son. "Where are you off to, hon?"

"I got a part-time job," he said, pointing to his hat.

"Giving tours of what, exactly?"

"Just some stupid tourist thing. You know that house on the border of Gothicville and Dystopia Z? They are opening it as a haunted house."

"And this job pays you money? You might be able to move out some-time soon?"

"Um, it's like an internship . . ." he trailed off.

"So no?"

The Internet Troll hung his head.

His mother sighed, "Well, let's go then. I'd love to see your new intern-ship!" Without waiting for her son to reply, Eugene's mom – Mrs. Troll? – slipped an overcoat over her housedress and walked out the front door.

"Parents are the worst," Eugene mumbled as he went to follow.

His mother's head reappeared in the doorway with a beaming smile. "What was that dear?" she asked in such a manner that said full-well she heard him.

"I'm dying of thirst," he said.

"Good thing I packed your favorite sippy cup!" she sang, pulling a Scooby-Doo decorated toddler cup, complete with a no-spill lid, from her large purse. "I'll drive you!"

"Yay," Eugene replied.

DEMONIC CARNIVAL

Eugene's mother parked the car a few meters from the 'Free Haunted House This Way' sign and turned off the ignition. "How exciting!" she cried. "My baby's first job. At only twenty-seven no less."

"Internship," the Internet Troll corrected.

"A job's a job, honey. Are you finished with your juice? Do you need any more snacks?" She lifted up her purse and shook it, the sound of crinkling paper, jingling coins, and clanging keys suggesting there may be no limit to the contents of said bag.

"I'm okay. Let me go greet the guests," he said, slipping out of the passenger seat.

The Internet Troll saw two creatures lined up at the sign and looked around. "Where is everyone else? I posted all over Blueit and 5Chon and I expected way more people to show up."

"Oy," called one of the creatures in line. He was a skeleton and had a very strong cockney accent. "Wotsit you say, lad? Wots this 5Chon nonsense?"

"It's only the coolest part of the Internet, Nigel. I don't expect you to know about it, you old sack of bones."

"Is that any way to treat your first customers?" the other creature asked. Well, this one was more of a person than a creature. At least as far as Eugene knew. Lilith was the Governess of Gothicville and possibly a vampire, but he wasn't sure. She was pale and gorgeous and was draped in a long black dress with a cloak. "We heard about this wonderful opening and just had to be the first to experience the haunted house. There are many in Gothicville, you know, but I can't wait to see what G and Z have put tougher for us."

"Missus Simmons," the skeleton said, tipping an invisible cap to Eugene's mother. "How might you be on this fine evenin', luv?"

"Oh Nigel." Mrs. Simmons flushed. "You know I just can't resist that accent."

"Mo-om!" Eugene cried. "Ugh. Gross. Fine. I guess you three will just have to be the first group."

Lilith, Nigel, and Mrs. Simmons stood in a group and gave Eugene their full attention.

"A few ground rules before we begin," he started. "First, touch whatever you like. This is a fully immersive experience. Don't worry about breaking things or defending yourself if you feel scared. It's perfectly okay."

"Well that is different," Lilith said with a smile. "Do go on."

"None of the plumbing is working properly, so if you have to use any restrooms, please do *not* flush the toilets. The cleaning crew will take care of it later."

"Yuck, but okay," Mrs. Simmons replied.

"Lastly, there is a good chance we may have to burn down the house to escape at the end. Don't worry, it's all part of the act. There are professionals in charge of this so don't be alarmed." He paused and giggled to himself. "Or four-alarmed, as it were."

None of the assembled 'tourists' laughed at the joke.

"You know, like a four-alarm fire?" he explained.

Nigel coughed. "We ain't missed the jest, lad. It jus' weren't funny isall."

"What would you know about humor? Your people think Monty Python is funny."

Nigel turned to Mrs. Simmons. "Permission to smack yer kid in the boat, mum? Full of porky pies, this one."

Mrs. Simmons paused for longer than Eugene was comfortable before answering. "Permission denied, luv."

"Roight then," the skeleton answered. He looked at the Internet Troll. "Outta respec' for your mum, you get one for free."

Eugene felt emboldened. "I don't even have a boat, you dumb limey."

Lilith appeared behind Eugene and whispered in his ear. "It means face, darling. And I wouldn't push your luck further. There's a reason I employ Nigel to guard the cemetery at the entrance to Gothicville. And it isn't his accent."

"Howdya what?" Eugene cried out. "Where did you come from? You were just over there," he said, pointing to the empty space next to Nigel and his mother where Lilith was previously standing silently.

"We all have our gifts, sweetie," she said through a grin. Her teeth gleamed brightly in the moonlight, especially the extra sharp canines.

"Um, this way please, folks," Eugene called. "We'll begin our tour of the haunted house on the porch." Eugene motioned for the three of them to follow him and they walked toward the house.

"He has no idea, does he?" Z said to G after the group was out of earshot.

"That idiot? He doesn't have any ideas that aren't fed to him by even bigger trolls through that Internet of his. Have you checked out that place?

It's a cesspool of echo chambers, driven by bots created by a handful of professional trolls to drive some rich guy's agenda. He's just a byproduct of the system." G answered.

"Yeah, so is poop."

G smiled. Or at least it seemed like he smiled because his eyeholes narrowed and his glasses rose a bit up off his non-existent nose. "An appropriate analogy, I'd say."

"Shall we observe our handiwork?" Z asked his partner.

"Indubitably!" G answered.

"Feel free to break that if you want," Eugene said to Lilith, who was sitting on a porch swing.

"Why would I?" she asked.

Eugene shrugged. "It's moving on its own. Might be haunted."

Lilith inspected the metal links of the swing. As they were on Z's side of the house and in a state of dereliction, the wood looked untreated and the links were rusted. Nothing suggested they were haunted or moving for any reason other than standard laws of physics.

"Looks like it might break on its own, dear," Mrs. Simmons said. "Not sure she needs to."

Eugene harrumphed and motioned to the front door. "Let's continue the tour inside." He reached down to grab the handle and screamed. The smell of seared flesh emanated from his hand. "Aaah!" The handle was lit up bright red, like it was about to catch fire.

"My poor darling!" Mrs. Simmons called. "Are you okay honey? What happened?"

Nigel sucked his teeth and said, "Looks like the handle o' that Roger Moore is right hot, mate. You best be careful. I hear this house is haunted."

Eugene glared at Nigel and kicked at the door on the half that was in Dystopia Z. It shattered easily. The red-hot metal doorknob fell to the ground. Eugene inspected the doorknob by pushing it with his foot and found that a curling iron was attached to the side of the handle that used to be the inside. "G and Z," he mumbled.

"What was that darling?" Lilith asked as she glided over the wrecked door into the entrance of the house.

"Just part of the tour!" Eugene said. He held up his hand, scorched with at least second-degree burns. "It's just makeup. Fooled you all didn't I?" He smiled and tried to hide his pain while flexing his hand to demonstrate how much it didn't actually hurt.

"Oy, good one mate," Nigel said with a laugh that chattered his skeletal jaw. He looked to Lilith and pointed a thumb at Eugene. "Gotta watch this one. He's quick, innit he?"

"That's my baby boy," Mrs. Simmons said beaming. "So clever."

Eugene turned from the three members of the tour and looked around the foyer. It was dimly lit. On the left side there was a grand spiral staircase with gothic carvings intricately woven through the dark wood. On the right, a rundown wooden staircase led into the basement of the Dystopia Z side of G and Z's home. In the middle of the entranceway, a rug that was clearly out of place sat. It looked like it belonged to G's gothic side of the house but it ran across the line separating Gothicville and Dystopia Z and didn't change appearance.

"Not this time," he said. He looked at Lilith. "After you Governess, lady's first. Just head over this rug to the beautiful staircase on your left and we'll continue the tour upstairs."

Lilith nodded her head slightly and walked over the carpet. It immediately gave way and revealed a giant hole in the floor. Lilith fell.

"Aiiiieeeee!" she cried, her scream fading as she fell for longer than seemed possible.

"Lilith!" Mrs. Simmons called, scrambling to the edge of the hole to peer down. "Eugene, what did you do?"

"I didn't do nothing! I said it was dangerous! Did I mention that there is a waiver I need you all to sign that removes any liability from the tour guide for this event?"

"Tell her that," Nigel said, pointing into the hole.

Eugene looked into the hole. "Governess?" He cleared his throat. "Lilith?"

The three remaining members of the group waited for a few seconds in silence. No response came from the hole. Lilith was gone.

In the basement of the house, G and Z stifled their laughter as Lilith floated safely and silently to the ground. She smiled at the ghost and zombie and whispered, "Does he really not know that I can fly?"

"He's not the sharpest bulb in the drawer," Z answered.

"Nor the brightest knife," G added.

Lilith shook her head. "So who's up next?"

"Nigel and a few of Z's friends from Dystopia Z," G said.

Z scratched his brain. "Let's see how dumb this kid can be."

"I'm sure she's fine," Eugene said. "In fact, I know she is. All part of the tour. We'll catch up with her later." He stood up from the hole and looked at the two paths before him: up into the gothic second floor or down to the basement of the run-down side. He chose down. At least no one would fall too far if they fell.

"Part of the tour, dear?" Mrs. Simmons asked.

"Yeah, mom. It's okay. Let's go. After you, Nigel," he said to the skeleton.

"Roight," Nigel replied. He clacked his way to the stairs. "You sure it's safe?"

Eugene paused for a moment. "Well, it's haunted. You might need to um, break things or something to defend yourself. I did warn you that."

"Right-o, mate." Nigel placed his foot on the first stair to go down and immediately lost his balance and tumbled down. As he crashed on each step, bits of bone flew off him, adding to the cacophony of bone on wood that was almost rhythmic until it ended in a pile of bone and wood at the base of the stairwell.

"Nigel!" Mrs. Simmons called.

"Oy," Nigel's skull called back. "I'm alright, Miss. Let me just pull myself together here," he joked. The various segments of bone began reassembling the skeletal frame that made up Nigel. Each of the pieces seemed to be able to help other pieces fit back together. "Hey, wot do you want, mate?"

"Nigel?" Mrs. Simmons called down the stairs. "Who are you talking to?"

"Just a few blokes making some gruntin' sounds and lookin' at ol' Nigel like a piece of meat. Oy, dead-for-brains, nuffin' but bones here."

Eugene stared down the dark stairwell and kneeled down to get a better look. He could see Nigel at the bottom, pretty much fully assembled now. He was holding up his hands defensively as a swarm of undead creatures from Dystopia Z collapsed on the skeleton.

"Aaaaah!" Nigel cried. "They be bitin' me bones!"

Eugene's eyes grew wide and he bit his lip. "Um," he stammered.

"P-p-art of the show, mom." He narrowed his eyes to peer through the darkness. Nigel had stopped screaming and was now standing in front of the other zombies. "See, he's okay!"

"Brains!" slurred Nigel.

"Oh my goodness," Mrs. Simmons cried out. "He's a zombie skeleton! What have you done Eugene? First Governess Lilith disappears into a hole and now Nigel is a zombie skeleton. Who ever heard of such a thing?"

"Mom! It's okay! They're idiots anyway. But I think the tour is over. We need to leave."

"We can't leave," Mrs. Simmons said. "We can't leave Nigel."

"Why not? He's just a dumb skeleton. Who cares?"

"I have to be with him," his mother answered. "There is something I never told you, Eugene. About your father."

Eugene bit his lip. "What about him? You said he died."

"He did," Mrs. Simmons said. "But his skeleton lived on," she said, her gaze moving from her son to Nigel, who was now standing at the top of the basement steps with blood dripping down his lips. Mrs. Simmons placed herself between Nigel and Eugene. "I won't let you kill your own son, zombie skeleton Nigel!"

Nigel looked at Eugene and then back to Mrs. Simmons. He shrugged and pounced on Eugene's mom, taking her to the ground with spurts of blood and screaming.

"Noooooooo!" the Internet Troll screamed and ran out of the house, narrowly avoiding the hole that Lilith fell through. He tripped over the broken front door and continued screaming as he ran in the general direction of his mom's house in Gothicville.

Nigel, Mrs. Simmons, Lilith, G, and Z stood on the front porch watching Eugene run into the horizon, still screaming loudly.

"Nice Darth Vader moment, Mrs. Simmons," G said.

Mrs. Simmons nodded and shrugged, "It was either that or an inappropriate joke about me and Nigel and something with bones involved."

"You sure you feel okay with helping us prank him?" Z asked.

"That little twerp? He deserves whatever he gets, all those comments about telling women to make sandwiches and whatnot. I hear him when he plays his video games."

Lilith grinned, baring her teeth again. "First class parenting, Mrs. Simmons."

"Thank you, Governess."

They all laughed at the events that took place and wondered if the Internet Troll would learn his lesson. They all assumed he wouldn't, but it was still fun.

"Hey Mrs. Simmons?" Z questioned.

"Yes, Z?"

"Your son owes us a door."

Everyone but Z began laughing again. In the distance, Eugene Simmons the Internet Troll disappeared over the horizon and was finally out of sight and earshot.

"No, seriously. He broke my door."

About the Author

Jeremy Rodden considers himself a dad first and an author second. He is the author of the middle grade/young adult cartoon fantasy Toonopolis series as well as numerous fantasy and science fiction stories in several anthologies. He can be found on his author website/blog at www.toonopolis.com or active on Facebook (facebook.com/toonopolis) and Twitter (@toonopolis).

Sometimes Ignorance
is not Bliss

K. Walker

Cold. Unthinking, I shot up in bed, coughing and spluttering. I cursed as my horns slammed against the low ceiling, the stone setting off sparks. Ducking my head, I wiped at my eyes. *Water?* I frowned, looking around immediately once my eyes were clear. My eyes fell on my brother, an impudent smirk on his face. He made no effort to hide the bucket he held in his hands, or that he thought my discomfort was highly amusing.

"Good morning, brother," he greeted cheerfully.

Growling, I leapt at him angrily, going for his throat. "I'm going to kill you!"

He leapt out of my reach, taunting me. "Oh, but mother will be sooo upset if you do."

"She's a demon; she'll get over it," I said flatly.

He paused, seeming to consider my words. "Hmm… well, she might, but you can't kill me anyway- we have an assignment."

Still angry, I couldn't stop myself from growling at him again. "And why would they bother giving us another assignment? You screwed up so badly on the last one, I'm surprised they didn't kill us for incompetence!"

That hit home, and his amusement faded a bit, but he was still cheerful as he replied. "Well, I gathered this was our second chance."

Suspicious, I scowled at him. "You mean *your* second chance! If you weren't my little brother, I'd have put us all out of our misery and killed you long ago! Why should I help you now? So you can bring my name down with yours again?"

Fidgeting uncomfortably, he looked away before replying. "It was their idea; they said you can put up with me better than most, and it's our turn anyway." When I started to shake my head, he continued quickly, sensing my refusal. "You have to! They're already expecting us, and my horns haven't grown in yet! They won't listen to me..."

"*Who* is expecting us?"

"Well... we've been ordered to help 3 younglings with lessons."

I felt my eyes narrow and I made a face. "Ugh. And just what are we supposed to teach them?"

He shrugged. "Possession mostly; just take them to the surface, guide them, let them practice. That sort of thing."

Thinking it over, I saw no other choice, and my shoulders slumped in dejection. Resigned to helping, I agreed. "Ok... Let's go... This had better not take too long..." I muttered as I followed him out of the cave.

They entered silently, taking the opportunity to study the young demons. From the look of it, one male was in the middle of boasting, trying to impress the lone female. The speaker stood on the left of the female, a greenish cast to his leathery skin; he stood tall, obviously trying to emphasize the barest beginnings of horns on either side of his forehead.

Hmm... he's not very old then. On the right, the second male, covered in blue-tinged scales, flexed his wings, trying to catch the female's eye and draw her attention away from the other male. *Likely also trying to keep her from noticing his horns haven't begun to grow yet,* I thought wryly. The female in question preened under the attention, her pink skin practically glowing as she smiled. I scowled as I looked at her. *Her horns haven't started growing either? Just how old are these 3? What did they do, stick us with the diaper brigade? They might have had their first lessons, but not much else...* I glanced at my brother; his oily skin gleamed a dull orange as he shifted under the weight of my gaze.

Rolling my eyes in annoyance, I took charge and strode up to the younglings, who had their backs facing the door. I growled and they jumped, silence descending as they turned. Seeing my horns, arcing over a foot from either side of my forehead, their eyes widened. Recognizing an Elder, they bowed in deference. My brother they ignored.

"So," I sneered. "I seem to have been given the task of teaching the lot of you. What are you meant to learn?" *Let's see if they're dumb enough to lie...*

The green-skinned male spoke up eagerly. "We are in the middle of possession, sir."

I scowled coldly, and he shrank back, fearing punishment. "Possession," I repeated, glaring at them. "And how is it you need help with that? All you do is concentrate, allow your bodies to fade into mist, then enter your target. It should be as easy as breathing!"

Dejected, the other male spoke. "We keep making mistakes, sir. Our attempts always go wrong for some reason, so they sent us back to practice."

"Practice?" I asked in disbelief. "For *possession?* You already learned the basics? And you actually need *practice?*" Three heads bowed in shame. My anger returning, I looked to my brother. "Just *what* did they say when they told you we had an assignment?"

He shrugged, unconcerned. "Not much. Just teach these 3 and we have permission to take them to the human realm for it."

I stared at him a moment longer, hoping for more, then turned back to look at the younglings. I sighed. *Why me?*

I stared into the scrying pool intently, searching for a good place to open a portal. The others stood at the entrance to the tiny cave, watching. I kept my wings folded tightly against my back, carefully trying to keep my horns away from the walls. *They need to widen this cave; I almost broke a horn the last time I was in here. That's the last thing I need; having those 3 younglings see that would be humiliating. I wonder if this is what a sardine feels like....* The pool finally cleared, showing me what looked to be a human carnival. I felt my lips stretch into a smile. *Perfect. There's plenty of targets there. Hopefully these brats will be quick. They can't possibly be THAT bad... I think I'll finish my nap first though... let my brother handle them for a while...they can always practice...*

When I went to rejoin them, I scowled when I saw the younglings weren't practicing their incorporeal forms as I had ordered before heading for my nap. In fact, it seemed as if they'd managed to talk my brother into a game of *tag* of all things. I paused in the archway, waiting for them to notice me, but then saw it was a lost cause. As I watched, my brother tripped, causing all of them to fall in a heap. Rolling my eyes at their stupidity, I stomped up to them, trying to restrain my anger.

"This does not look like practice," I growled, carefully enunciating each word.

Caught off guard, the female froze, the males went pale, and my brother flinched guiltily. He was the first to recover though, trying to roll over so he could get to his feet. It was then I realized that in my anger, I'd made a mistake; I had gotten too close. Unable to turn completely, he ended up knocking into me, and I fell over on top of them. The students, believing it was an attack, immediately tried to get away, and chaos ensued.

A hand caught in my robe, the claws tearing into it and becoming trapped. That only made the owner of the hand panic and start flailing madly. The panic quickly spread to the others, and soon limbs were flying in all directions. One, likely an elbow, hit me in the nose hard, and blood spurted. The scent of blood only made everyone more frantic. With a great heave and the sound of tearing fabric, I managed to wrench myself out of the pile, landing heavily. Assessing the damage, I noted I had bruises everywhere, my nose still bleeding, and my eye had begun to swell. Checking my horns, I was relieved to find they remained intact. Looking down though, I cringed; my robes were torn in several places. *Great. Now I have to change... these brats may be the death of me,* I thought sourly.

I stood up, painfully aware I no longer looked even remotely dignified. By now, the others had managed to untangle themselves and were taking stock; none had faired as bad as I had. *They practically look pristine compared to the way I feel.* The girl was the first to look up at me and she gasped, drawing the others' attention. All three younglings scrambled to their feet, bowing and trying to apologize all at once. My brother actually laughed, then tried to change it into a cough when I glared at him.

"Silence!" I roared. Aside from my brother, who was still 'coughing,' they froze. "If this is any indication of how little you want to learn, it's no wonder you need *practice*." I spat at them, no longer trying to conceal my anger. "This will be the one and only time I take you brats to the surface; after that, you'll be someone else's problem. I have chosen the location. Get ready."

"Sir," the girl whispered. Turning a cold glare on her, I waited, hardly believing she'd dared to speak. She flinched but persisted. "Our names-" Rolling my eyes in scorn, I cut her off. "I don't give a damn what your names are! In fact- you are now A, B, and C!" I announced, pointing to each in turn.

The green-skinned male was A, the 2nd male B, and the girl ended up with C. Not waiting for a reply, I turned away, opening the portal. Slowly an image formed, of a dark, out-of-the-way corner. Boxes of all shapes and sizes were scattered about. A carousel horse even leaned against the wall. Beyond, people walked past, laughing and talking animatedly, though we heard nothing. As the late afternoon sun began to set, bright, colorful lights could be seen, growing brighter with each passing minute. No one seemed to notice the portal.

Forgetting his shame, Boy A jumped around, clapping excitedly. "Where is that? And why are there so many people?"

Shooting him a glare, I replied anyway. "It's what the humans call a carnival. As you can see, you have plenty of humans to choose from. Now go," I continued, gesturing at the portal. "And work together! This isn't a competition! Do not be too eager either; wait for the perfect opportunity to strike and you will avoid mistakes. I will come to check on your progress in a couple hours. Until then, you'll have only each other."

"Wait, what? Aren't you supposed to come with us?" The girl asked nervously.

Making an effort to reign in my temper, I smiled evilly and pointed to the portal. After some hesitation, one-by-one they went through. My brother followed them, and I brought up the rear, cloaking my presence as I closed the gateway behind me.

Once through, I stepped back to make sure I was out of the way so I could watch them closely. I scowled. *I wanted to see if they could actually work together, but it isn't looking too promising. I've seen enemies get along better...*I sighed, my eyes narrowing further as I watched. *Make that enemies with blood feuds...* They began to argue heatedly, standing at the alcove's exit. People were eying them askance and giving them a wide berth, but they didn't seem to care; my brother just stood there looking stupid. Boy A apparently wanted to go right, while Boy B was just as determined to go left. To give the girl *some* credit, she was trying to get them to compromise, but she may as well have been talking to a wall.

Eventually, A got tired of arguing and grabbed the girl's arm, trying to pull her behind him. Of course, B wasn't about to let him get away with that, and he grabbed her other arm. I'm sure my brother's expression matched mine as we stood dumbfounded, watching as they actually played tug-of-war. The look on the girl's face was priceless. *I guess it doesn't matter how many compliments she gets; she won't stand for being pulled apart at both ends.* She wrenched her arms away, and both boys over-balanced and fell flat on their faces. The girl smiled, then left on her own. *I really can't blame her for that...* The boys were slow to recover, and she was long gone by the time they looked for her. They scowled at each other, then stomped off in opposite directions. *So much for working together.* Taking the chance, I conjured a new robe, pulling it on as my brother joined me. *Of course, he was strong enough to sense me; the younglings didn't even think to look.*

"Well that could have gone better," he said.

"Shut up." I settled back to wait, and my brother did the same.

The newly designated 'A' stormed away angrily, not caring where he was going. People hurriedly dodged out of his way, cursing him as he passed. He was so angry he didn't even notice when he bumped into a man, causing him to dump his slushie all over his girlfriend. Her white blouse was ruined, now dyed a bright red. His apologies fell on deaf ears as she began to yell at him, while her face and hair dripped in shades of red. *That bastard. Who does he think he is? I got there first, so I should've had first chance at the girl! He should never have stuck his big nose in! She likely wouldn't be interested in him anyway; he looks like a walking corpse! Ugh... I wish I knew her name. Somehow, I never got around to asking...*

Lost in his thoughts, he was startled when he ran into what felt like a wall. He looked up to see a man stumbling back, turning to face him once he'd recovered. Clearly a hippie, the man lowered his colored glasses to see better, only mildly offended.

DEMONIC CARNIVAL

"Dude! Watch where you're going, ya?" The man blinked, then squinted, getting a closer look. "Ya know full body paint is bad, ya? Your skin's gotta breathe, man!"

Growling in disgust, he pushed past the man, only to freeze at his parting words.

"Hey, I'd pick a different color than green though, ya? It kinda looks like ya jumped in a pile o' poo!"

It looks...WHAT? Furious, he spun around as those nearby snickered, his hands balled into fists, but the man was gone. *I'll show him! I'll show all of them!* Looking around, his eyes fell on the strong man game. Several people waited their turn, one of which was a man with huge, bulging muscles. *He must be at least 7 feet tall...* he couldn't help but smile. *Perfect. He'll do nicely.* It was the man's turn next. He closed his eyes to focus, and when he stepped up to the mark, he rushed in eagerly. He felt the familiar tingle as the possession took hold, but then everything went dark.

'Girl C' fumed, threading her way through the crowd. She got a few odd looks, but no one bothered her. *How dare they? Flirting is one thing, but touching? No way! Surely, they know I have standards! Which don't include males who can't even manage basic skills. The teacher might have been a good choice, but he gave me a letter for a name. I should've gotten 'A' at the very least.* I scowled at the insult. *No... I'm sure I can find a ton of better options.*

Oooh... speaking of... Her anger was forgotten as a couple approached her. When they passed, she followed, as if pulled along by a string. *That is one yummy male. Dark hair, bright blue eyes... yes, please! The girl isn't too thrilling, but I can put up with her for a chance at him.* Keeping pace with them, she made sure to stay out of sight so they wouldn't notice her. They passed several likely games before the couple finally chose one. *Ring Toss... couldn't they have chosen something more fun?* She watched them, thinking hard. *I guess I can possess a prize and have them bring me home, but that stupid blonde will have to win first... Ooh I know what I can do! This is sure to work! I'll be out of these extra classes in no time...* Trying not to squeal in triumph, she closed her eyes.

Sometimes Ignorance is not Bliss by K. Walker

Walking along dejectedly, Boy B searched for the girl in vain. *Where'd she go? I thought I saw her come this way...* Turning in circles, he became thoroughly lost, and still there was no sign of her. *This place is a maze...I guess I'll have to get to work; wasting more time would probably be a bad idea. It would have been nice to have her help though.* He sighed, searching for a target.

Well... I don't think trying to possess a human directly would be wise... at least not for me. Let's see... Wandering aimlessly, he finally stopped next to the dart game. Brightly colored balloons covered the back wall. *Maybe if I focus on one of those darts I can enter a human if they cut their finger on it...* He stood there, unseeing, but nothing else came to mind. *Why do I have to be so bad at this? It should be so easy...*He shuddered. *I need to pass too, or mom will make me dress up in that ridiculous clown suit again. And there's no telling where she'd send me if I fail this time. New York was bad enough.* Nervous, he couldn't stop himself from chewing on his lip. *Ok... it isn't the greatest plan, but I guess it's better than nothing.* His decision made, he took deep breaths, his gaze never wavering from the darts. *Here goes nothing...*

A couple hours later, the demon brothers stood on a hill in the center of the carnival.

"They should've had plenty of time by now. Let's see how they did..."

My brother nodded in agreement. Remaining in the shadows, they scanned the area, pointing out the locations where they sensed demonic energy. Surprisingly they'd all ended up on the south side, not too far from one another in spite of having set off in different directions.

The first they focused on was the Ring Toss game, on the far left, where a crowd had formed. Joining the crowd, they made their way to the front. It looked like there was a competition going. A human girl was hitting her targets every time, while an older guy, red-faced by this point, was missing entirely. A pile of stuffed animals lay at the girl's side. *That's odd.* As I watched, the girl made another throw. It was a completely wild toss and should have missed by a mile, but amazingly she scored again. *Don't tell me...* I focused on the energy once more, and sure enough, it emanated from the pegs. This close, I could tell it was the female youngling.

She possessed the... I shared a look with my brother, who had realized the same thing.

"Did she really possess game pegs?" he asked.

"It looks that way," I replied irritably. "I guess she forgot she was supposed to choose a human target." I scowled as the human girl got another prize and the crowd cheered.

"Well..." my brother said, his voice weak. "Let's... go see how the others did... maybe they fared better..."

Shaking my head, I followed him to the next place, which ended up being Boy B. A child of about 10 stood in front of the dart game. Uncertain of where our student was, we watched the boy throw. When the dart hit the board, our eyes widened as we heard a yelp.

The boy giggled, looking at his parents. "This game is great! They've never made sounds before!" he said cheerfully.

Shaking our heads, we left without a word.

The third area had another large crowd; we found we couldn't push our way through this time, so we were forced to retreat to the hill and watch from afar. Once we had, all we could do was stare in disbelief. Human after human swung a mallet down onto a metal plate, apparently testing their strength, as it was labeled 'Strong Man.' But every time the mallet struck, a high-pitched cry of pain sounded, along with a roar of laughter from the crowd.

I facepalmed, feeling a headache coming on as I turned to my brother. "How long did you say we had them for?"

"Until they learn," he replied miserably.

Glancing back towards the students, I frowned. "What if they don't learn?"

I looked back to my brother in time to see him shrug helplessly.

I thought for a moment. "We could always say they died in an explosion."

His face hopeful, he considered the suggestion. "What would cause all 3 of them to die in 1 explosion?"

"Extreme stupidity."

"Hmm..."

ABOUT THE AUTHOR

K. Walker has always wanted to be a writer. She has a huge imagination, helped along by her love of reading and the written word. With the dictionary she carries around in her head, she also makes a good editor. K. has always wanted to spread her love of reading by writing her own stories for others to enjoy. She'll write about anything that catches her interest. Her favorite genre to write is fantasy and anything that makes her imagination soar, because there's no telling what will pop into her head. She loves to read Sci-Fi, Fantasy, Paranormal Romance, and even a bit of Mystery and Horror, but Non-Fiction books have been known to put her to sleep. Her imagination gets pulled in so many directions, her mind is pure chaos, so this is the first story she's managed to finish, though she hopes to one day finish the other stories bouncing around inside her head. She also enjoys spending time on games and will most often be seen playing League of Angels with her friends when she isn't reading, editing, researching, or trying to write down all the ideas clamoring for her attention.

A Tasty Festival

Angelique Fawns

Stacey sat on her porch waiting for something exciting to happen. Life gets so boring in a small town for an eight-year-old, and she wants something more adventurous to do rather than just ride her bike.

"Stacey, you run around so much, I swear you have ants in your pants," her mom says.

Though she has given her underwear a good look, she's never found any ants. She's about to go to the backyard and see if she can really dig all the way to Australia when a loud rumbling on the road catches her attention. Some large transport trucks are rumbling by pulling and carrying carnival rides. The noise makes her want to cover her ears, but her eyes goggle at the amazing cargo. A green dragon head grins at her from the back of one, its twisty roller coaster body in a heap behind it. The ugly head of a fortune teller leers at her from its glass box, surrounded by bags of enormous stuffed animals.

She jumps up and runs down the road after the trucks. That's right! This weekend is the Sunderland Maple Syrup Festival, and it's her absolute favorite time of the year. The first weekend of April is full of cotton candy, local bands, frozen maple syrup on a stick, and of course the rides! Forget her silly bike, she is going to go on the Ferris wheel, the Spider, and maybe even a roller coaster.

This year she knows she is going to make the height line; she just had a growth spurt and eight is so much older than seven. She's sick to death of only being allowed to go on the baby rides. If she has to ride in a little choo choo train one more time, her brain will go right off its track! Stacey giggles at her pun and coughs on the exhaust from the trucks when another kid joins her.

"Hey, the Carnies are in town! The Carnies are here! They're going to sneak into your house at night and kill you," Hudson, the boy from down the street shouts.

Stacey doesn't like Hudson. He likes to tease all the girls and hangs with the tough crowd of hockey boys. His blonde hair is always messy, and he smells like old soccer shoes. Hudson pulls on her curly black hair at school and Stacey wishes he would just fall in a hole and tumble all the way to Australia himself.

Her Dad is a quiet man who was born down under in Sydney but met her Mom on an artist's work visa and got married instead of going home. He's a carpenter who creates kangaroos and koala bears out of wood stumps and sells them to rich people as lawn ornaments. He always has a booth at the Sunderland Maple Sugar Festival and sales of his creations are usually brisk. This is why Stacey knows she will be seeing all those rides on the back of the truck at the fair, the family never misses it.

Hudson and Stacey both stop running after the truck and stare at each other. She doesn't know whether she should run from him before he tries to give her a noogy or stick around to see if he pulls a stupid stunt. Last time she saw Hudson, he was trying to ride his neighbour's pot-bellied pig. It somehow ended with him in a mud puddle and the pig on his back chewing his hair. She laughed for days.

"Hey Stace! Come with me, I've got something super cool to show you!" Hudson says tossing his water bottle back and forth. "The coolest thing ever."

"Yah, what?" Stacey mutters, curiosity tickling.

Her brain tells her to stay away from the bad boy, but she's bored. Hudson is never boring. She remembers when he came running into the school gym during an assembly with baby skunks under his arms. Total chaos. It was awesome. The gym still smells.

"I can't even explain it, it's so rad, you just have to come," Hudson grabs her arm.

Well, curiosity killed the cat, but satisfaction brought it back, so she follows him.

"This better not end with me muddy, stinky, or bleeding, and I can't be gone long. It's almost dinner time."

They walk a couple blocks to the ice arena and a little playground. At the edge of the teeter-totters Hudson shows her the most enormous ant hill. Little red dots scurry back and forth keeping their metropolis fed and growing.

She knells down, glad for her tight joggers, she doesn't need any of these getting in her pants, "Look at all the darling busy things."

Hudson walks away collecting little bits of tree branch and sticks.

"What are you doing?"

Not answering, he piles them on the hole at the top of the hill. Digging into his jeans he pulls out a matchbook and lights the tinder. A bit of flame immediately catches with a small whoosh. The ants scurry everywhere, racing for their wee lives.

"Hudson! Don't burn them! That's terrible," she huffs at the flames, but can't seem to blow them out. She contemplates grabbing a few bigger red ants to slide into his underwear. Hopefully they are the biting kind.

"Firetruck 81, responding to a 9-1-1 call!" Hudson bellows.

Picking up a water bottle he tossed on the dirt, he dumps the liquid on his small fire. With a hiss it extinguishes.

"See? I'm a hero," Hudson says proudly, "I saved the big ant condominium."

Stacey stares at him. She never should have followed a known sociopath.

"Hey, what's that over there? By the corn field?" Hudson points at a metal structure sitting at the edge of the field near last year's corn husks.

She stands up to look, "I'm not sure. Doesn't look like it belongs. Is someone dumping garbage?"

They walk over to it, and gap at the thing. It's a square box with roll bars over head and a pea soup green seat with torn cushions. Little doors are attached to each side with grotesque clown faces painted on them. Stacey is NOT a fan of clowns after watching Stephen King's IT one night with an overly permissive babysitter. Sometimes you think you are grown up enough, and you just aren't. She doesn't even like red balloons anymore.

"It looks like part of a Ferris Wheel," she says getting a little closer, "how would it get here?"

"It's cool," Hudson shouts, pulling open the little side door and hopping onto the seat.

With a clang the clown face panel swings shut.

A Tasty Festival by Angelique Fawns

"BLURP," a big sucking sound comes out of the cab.

Hudson screams as his butt sinks into the seat. The green cushion opens like a huge mouth and Hudson is now bent over at the waist with his legs and arms sticking out in front of him. He looks ridiculous, and Stacey wants to giggle at the way his eyes are popping out of his face, and the small "O" of his mouth open in surprise.

"Is this another of your stunts? It's better than pig riding."

"Get me out of here! Get help," Hudson yells as he sinks in even further until just his shoes and hands are visible.

Then it's too late for help, Hudson is gone, and the green seat looked solid again. Stacey takes a few steps back. This is crazy. She didn't just see a boy eaten by a Ferris Wheel cab, did she?

"BURP", the green seat flaps open and shut.

She did.

Stacey turns and runs as fast as her legs can take her. When she gets back to the playground she turns and looks back for the carnivorous carnival seat, but the metal thing and Hudson are gone. She walks home quickly trying to figure out what to do about this. No one is going to believe her story.

Once she came screaming in from the back yard, "Dad there is a huge rattlesnake in the yard! It almost got me!"

After her father spent an hour searching through his gardens with a pitchfork and a can of Raid, she had to fess up.

"Maybe it was only a garter snake, it just looked like it was a rattlesnake."

She was grounded for an entire week for something called "hyperbole." She's still not exactly sure what that means, but she knows her parents roll their eyes if she tells too fantastic a tale.

When she gets home her mother has dinner on the table, so Stacey doesn't say anything. She gags when she tries to eat the green pea soup. Visions of a little Hudson swimming around in the green mush makes her stir her spoon around trying to squash him.

There is a knock at the door, and her mom opens it.

"Have you seen Hudson, he hasn't come home for supper, which is unusual for him," the blonde lady with her hair sprayed into a massive pouf asks.

"Stacey, do you know where Hudson is?" her mom calls over her shoulder.

She imagines telling the two ladies that Hudson has been sucked into another world through the green seat of an old Ferris wheel. Her parents might ground her until she's old enough to go to university.

"Mom, I have NO idea where Hudson could be."

Lying in bed that night, she half convinces herself she dreamed the whole encounter. She'd rather think of fun things, like riding the green dragon roller coaster! She falls into a deep sleep...

The next day her family packs up the van with a bunch of Dad's creations, and Stacey hops in the back with the wooden kangaroos, possums, and wombats. Hudson probably stumbled home last night after playing a mean trick on all of them. Imagine believing a nasty piece of carnival ride ate him! She helps set up the tables and sculptures, but her tummy is getting bubbly thinking about the rides.

"Can I go explore now?"

"Sure thing, honey, just take my cell phone and call your Dad if you need anything or get into trouble. Keep an eye out for Hudson," her Mom says pulling a toque onto Stacey's head. Great, now she looks like a cone head. If she lived in Australia, she wouldn't have to wear silly toques, but, the April breeze is cool and blows last year's leaves up and down the street.

She skips away, listening to the band warming up, and watching the big draft horses taking their first visitors for a tour in a hay wagon. A big pot of maple syrup is boiling by the old church. The sweet smell tickles her nostrils. The midway should be open, and she's got to double check her height.

The main town parking lot has been transformed into a wonderland of fun, food, and midway rides. Stacey watches the green dragon roller coaster clack by and can't wait to try it out. The ticket booth has the colored height tester. She runs over and lines up beneath it. Yes! A Carnie with a bald head and toothless smile wordlessly hands her the bracelet that means she can go on anything. The line-up for the roller coaster and the spider are pretty long, so she walks over to the Ferris wheel, which has no one waiting.

The old ride towers into the air, with the metal seats with green cushions and clowns painted on the sides swinging in the wind. A cheery version of "Pop Goes the Weasel" plays out of tinny speakers. Stacey comes to a dead stop, her heart threatening to jump up and run out of her mouth. She's afraid Hudson might pop out of one of the cars.

Another Carnie with a dirty ball cap and patched overalls turns and looks at her.

"Hey Girlie! Want to be the first one on? I see you're tall enough to ride!"

Backing away, Stacey turns and sprints out of the midway. Maybe she's had enough excitement for the moment. She knows one thing is for sure, she is NEVER going to ride the Ferris wheel.

ABOUT THE AUTHOR

Angelique Fawns is a journalist who began her career writing about naked cave dwellers in Tenerife and parasailing in Australia. She has a full-time job creating commercials for Global TV in Toronto; and lives on a farm with her husband, daughter, cows, horses, fainting goats and an attack llama. You can find her fiction in Ellery Queen Mystery Magazine, The Gateway Review: A Journal of Magical Realism, The Corona Book of Ghost Stories, Strange Women in Horror, Accursed, EconoClash and Pulp Modern.

www.fawns.ca
@Raingirl51

HERE'S TO THE FUTURE

Jessica Chaleff

alliope music traveling softly throughout the nearby town could only mean one thing for the young and old alike: The Carnival was back. It granted a small escape from everyday woes with overpriced food and take apart thrill rides no one has ever heard of before. Between the rides, fried fat, and chances to win dollar store stuffed toys, were the booths and tents, willing to provide entertainment with a higher price tag. Brant could never save enough money to fully enjoy the Carnival before, but this year he saved enough to experience everything at least once and have enough fried treats to make his stomach declare secession later on.

This year was different. He'd be starting College in a couple of months, and this was his last chance to be a child. Sure, beating a six-year-old at ring toss for a stuffed Unicorn wasn't exactly becoming of an eighteen-year-old, but it was Brant's last hurrah before succumbing to adulthood and everything that comes with it.

There was one part of the Carnival that bothered Brant. The employees. There were the ones who ran the booths, and shows, and sold the food, but then there were the ones who sold the little trinkets. Brant could tell they didn't want to be there, and yet, they returned every year, selling the same cheaply made items, with the same glazed over look in their eyes. They didn't look at you, but past you, and mumbled when they spoke. However, this year, he wouldn't let them bother him. This is the last year he would attend the Carnival and allow himself to act as childish as possible.

The entrance was as cheesy as ever. A towering, plywood clown, looking down at those who dared to enter through his open mouth. It needed some sanding, Brant noticed, as a large splintered piece of wood nearly caught his shirt. The ticket booth had no line, but the cries of joy boomed from within the carnival. Brant approached the candy cane striped booth, and eavesdropped on the conversation between a young woman, and the top-hatted owner of the Carnival.

"I realize the carnival employs the same people every year, but is there any sort of openings available?" The woman asked sweetly.

"I'm sorry, but we don't have any job openings this summer." There was a glint in his eye. "There is, however, one position we may have room for."

"Oh?" She asked hopefully.

Brant stepped in. "I think she's way overqualified."

The woman turned on him, her eyes wide. "Please don't say that. I need to start saving money for College."

"What's your name?"

"Amanda."

"Look at them, Amanda." Brant pointed out all the trinket salesmen. "They look dead, boring, like they've been in storage all year. You? You have more life in you than all of them put together. They don't have much of a future if they keep returning here. There are better places for a Summer job than here."

Amanda smiled. "Maybe you're right. I just thought it would be fun to work at the Carnival."

"Rose colored glasses." Brant smiled back.

"Thanks." She glanced awkwardly at the man in the booth, before walking through the clown's mouth.

Brant produced five dollars from his pocket and slipped it through the hole in the window. "One ticket please."

The top-hatted man took the money, and slipped Brant the ticket, but not letting go quite yet. His lips pulled back over his yellow teeth into a gruesome smile. "I don't suppose you would like to fill that position, would ya?"

Brant nearly fell back as he won the ticket tug of war. "Yeah, right. I've a future. I mean, look at that one. He's in his mid-thirties and still doling out light-up pinwheels. I'm just here to get in some fun before I head off to College. And unlike Miss Amanda, I'd rather work elsewhere if I needed a job."

The man continued to smile. "Suit yourself."

As Brant walked away, the top-hatted man exited his booth, and snapped his fingers. The noise was silent to all the guests, but alerted the main employees of the Carnival, especially the one in the small, purple tent. The man beckoned over the mid-thirties gent selling pinwheels, and whispered something in his ear. Grunting in response, the trinket salesman trudged to his next destination.

Brant realized he was being stared down by varying booth owners, but the smell of fried dough was overpowering, and quickly turned his paranoia into a ferocious hunger. He wasn't exactly proud of the powdered sugar that covered his face, or the fact he had to wipe away dribbles of oil – his stomach will surely make him regret this choice later. With a quick check of his watch, he began to think of how many activities could he complete before the Freak Show performance at three o'clock. Perhaps the Tilt-a-Whirl, and a few rounds of the ball toss. *Sounds about right.* As Brant dodged his way around screaming kids covered in cotton candy, he found himself drawn to the sight of an elderly woman, sitting all alone in front of a ratty, small tent.

The tent could have been considered nice looking at one point, but the yellow stars have faded into puke colored smears, and the outer façade had been shredded by time. Out of all the attractions at the Carnival, this one had been steered clear of, which was surprising, considering the Fortune Teller Tent was always a popular spot. Spotting Brant and feeling his gaze, the woman looked up, and smiled, bearing quite a few missing teeth.

"Care to step inside, young man?"

"Well," Brant shuffled his feet, "it's... it's not really my style."

"I haven't had a visitor all day. Would you mind humoring an old lady? No charge."

No charge, eh? Brant felt his Carnival savings in his pocket. A free attraction fits the budget alright. "Sure. Why not?"

The old woman, clearly embracing the old Gypsy stereotype in her appearance, stood up with amazing ease, and pulled back the entrance flaps, releasing a perfume of, of... Brant couldn't discern *what* is was, but it was comforting, and the best scent he's ever had the pleasure to be graced with. She pulled out the stool at the small table, gesturing for the boy to sit, before taking her place across from him. The crystal ball was less than impressive – surely something from a Halloween prop shop. The smell of a fog machine was surely to come. The Gypsy woman held her gnarled fingers over the small crystal orb, and closed her eyes, as if trying to will the orb to light up. It didn't. And there wasn't a fog machine in sight. Brant sighed. *Not much of a fortune teller vibe in here.* He felt her fingers curl around his hand, yelping at the sudden grip she had on him. He looked up only to be met with her cloudy eyes.

"You have no future." She croaked.

With those words, the inside of the tent had changed. It appeared worn down, on the edge of collapse, and that once comforting smell became... became... some sort of combination of bad breath, dust, and a hint of something decomposing in the background. Every spot in the Carnival was ridiculously made-up to help people escape reality, but this? Brant was suffocated by the moment, as this rip-off quickly became a reality check. He wanted to be a kid one last time, and now, even once wonderful things have turned sour as this old hag kept croaking on and on the same words: You have no future. You have no future. You have no future. You have no future.

With a quick jolt backwards, Brant was able to free his hand, but couldn't will himself to leave the bizarre situation. The Gypsy woman stood up and made her way to the curtain partition at the back of the tent, pulling it back to reveal that no-life, mid-thirties employee Brant was fixated on earlier. The box of cheap pinwheels clattered to the floor, as the man staggered forward, taking the Gypsy's place in the seat at the table – his glazed over eyes slid from their transfixed point in space, and decided to settle on the now glowing crystal ball. The horrifying hag of a Gypsy approached the poor man and held out her hand. Ethereal glowing tendrils seeped from every orifice on the man's face.

The Gypsy shot out her other hand and grabbed the back of Brant's head, forcing him to face the crystal ball, and stare into the increasingly, intensifying light as it absorbed whatever was spilling from the man's face. Brant felt his body lock up, unable to move as his eyes remained fixated on the light until it faded into unnerving darkness. The former employee of the perennial carnival was now a dried husk and sagged to the ground. The Gypsy removed her hand from the back of Brant's head and gestured to the box of cheap, light-up pinwheels on the floor. She turned to a figure in the entrance of her tent.

"You picked a good one, sir. He'll last for a few decades." The Gypsy smiled, bearing her few and far between rotting teeth.

The Carnival owner grinned back.

The crowds were back again the very next day, spending fortunes on fried foods and rigged games. Laughter mingled with calliope music and Barkers calling out for audience participation. Among the returning guests was Amanda, with a few of her friends. She loved the Carnival, but she supposed that boy from the other day was right – working there might ruin the magic. Her friends were dragging her to all the games, enticed by the Barkers, and begging her to pay for each round. However, all the lights and sounds couldn't distract her from observing those lost souls selling trinkets. That boy had told her they had no future, and the more she watched them, the more it appeared to ring true. They all looked lost. There was no hope in their eyes. As her friends argued over who truly won the ring toss, Amanda found herself drawn to one particular trinket salesman, selling light-up pinwheels. Her head bowed in disappointment upon viewing the figure. Apparently that boy just wanted the job for himself.

About the Author

Jessica Chaleff is an avid lover of all things horror and sci-fi. These genres tend to blossom through writing, as well as art. She currently lives at home, hunched over a laptop, constantly writing. Jessica can be found interacting with people through social media almost daily! You can find her on Twitter, Facebook, Instagram, YouTube, and even Etsy. Just look up TimeLassCreations, or TheTimeLass, and look for a bow-tied clock a bowler hat!

BEAUTY FOREVER MORE

Ross Ellison

Sam checked his phone and pinched his cheeks twice to make sure he stood awake. No trickery remained to deceive him! He had secured a date with one of the most beautiful women in school. No matter how lame his method had been, he had succeeded.

Though a junior in high school, Sam loomed only average in height. Built halfway between football player and scrawny nerd, there had been issues with him standing out. Many of the underclassman had distinguished themselves, and yet here he simply existed. However, Sam prepared mentally for a date with *her*.

All of this had been possible because he shared a name with this lovely lady. Samantha existed right out of a fairy tale. Not the princess of course, but the beautiful enchantress of the story. Sam admired her hair, silky and perfect from a distance. This lovely lady of the night had an Elvira poster in her locker telling a gleam of her personality.

But when he had asked her on a date, pressured on by one of the few friends he had, the smile he received made his soul melt away. The text on his phone informed him that she would be blessing him again with her presence soon.

Now, for the date itself. Given Samantha's love of darkness, from her makeup, hair color, and interests, Sam had found the perfect place for an unforgettable first date. Perhaps the average man could not win her over with skills he lacked. But tonight, he would prove his courage.

DEMONIC CARNIVAL

A dark mistress needed a brave man to complete her after all. Reading the words again that she had sent to him made his heart race. *The old carnival site? The one that is supposed to be haunted? That sounds exciting! I'll see you at 5!* She had left him a winky face emoji too. Best not for him to read into that too much. His brain scrambled nonstop anyway.

Compared to the courage of speaking openly to this unapproachable beauty, going to a ruined carnival sight appeared to be a simple matter. The place gave him the creeps though. Of course, coming here after the sunset had been her idea.

Winter attempted to get in his way, but Sam wore his warmest sweater. Though when he turned towards the parking lot and saw a second car approaching, he regretted wearing clothes that absorbed his sweat.

A chill wind made the Junior shiver as another person came out of the car. Tall and lanky, a skeleton of an adult shuffled towards him. Only when he had been spotted did Sam remember that where he currently found himself, sat behind a fence. A fence he had illegally crossed!

"What are you doing here young man?" At first the teen thought trouble had arrived. But on a second listen, the mysterious adult simple posed a question. His tone more curious than upset in truth. On a gut feeling that lying to this person would be a mistake, the reality spilled out.

"I asked a beautiful woman on a date and decided to take her here to show that I am brave."

"Well spoken." The mysterious man answered. Standing next to this person created the shocking realization in how vast the... "I was about to call the authorities, but I like your answer, so I will forgive you." Looking down on Sam, this man seemed to be judging and summing him up at the same time.

"I'm- I'm Sam." He outstretched his hand to the stranger in hopes that respect would prevent him from changing his mind.

"Ah yes, my name's Samuel. Samuel Crum. I own these grounds."

What a strange turn of events. Instead of being kicked off the property, the owner told him instead to take a tour around. So long as they didn't break anything, there stood little harm in a couple thrill seekers living out a horror movie in safety. Samuel grinned and went off into the ruins of the carnival. Sam realized after he left that this person numbered three in individuals who shared a similar name.

Shaking his head to clear away his fears of this odd coincidence, he jumped when a warm hand touched his shoulder. His head screamed in terror, but his nose wanted to stay a while. The scents that tickled him made it obvious who has surprised him.

"Did I scare you?" Samantha whispered into his ear.

Sam turned to face this beautiful enchantress. Apparently, she possessed stealth skills too. With their faces almost touching, he slowly backed up. While he did, the teen had to keep reminding himself to look into her eyes. Not anywhere else, especially not her chest. Yes, definitely not there.

I am not a pervert!

Things not helping included a black silky dress that seemed to be an extension of her hair. Mixed with red lipstick, the color scheme made his heart flutter. How could he help himself to such thoughts!

This isn't fair.

"Are you already frightened?" She teased.

Did women do this on purpose?

"No." He avoided lying. Intimidated and being frightened were not the same thing. Right?

"Well, my courageous escort, let's go inside!" He didn't even get a chance to tell Samantha about Samuel before the two crossed the gates. She never even asked why the gate stood open.

"Where would you like to go first?" Sam asked looking in all cardinal directions. Most of the rides looked dangerous to even stand near. Only a fool would want to ride one. The roller coaster had holes in its tracks. No complete circuit to be found in the nearby go-cart track either.

"Let's go over there!" The enchantress had long nails too. They were an extension of her beautiful figure. Truly an average man like him had no place being near her much less on a date. Yet she had said yes. Sam needed to man up.

Finally looking past his date, the teen saw what she had found. The only stable looking ride within eyesight loomed a carousel.

"Do you think it works?" He asked, trying to show courage.

"We can find out." She flashed a soul crushing smile and dragged him along. But she held to him tightly to give him the illusion of being in control.

Her perfume threatened to overwhelm him completely. Certainly, she's a supernatural witch had come to claim him as her own. And he had brought her to this carnival! In the horror movie, this would be a terrible thing for him.

"I know you're afraid." She whispered to him. "So, let me give you some courage." Warmth on his cheek made him gasp as he realized that Samantha had just given him his first kiss. "You are braver than you think."

Wondering if it would be gross if he never washed that cheek again, Sam's foot banged into metal and called him back to earth. "Let's check if it's safe." he informed the enchantress who still clung to his arm.

"What's the worst that could happen?" Samantha asked as she looked around at the merry go round. "This isn't a roller coaster or thrill ride. No drops to worry about. At worst the machine brakes and we get off. She let go of his arm and wandered towards one of the nearby horses.

Something seemed strange about this ride. Perhaps his encounter with Samuel had shaken his body more than he wanted to admit. But Sam kept quiet. His date had called him heroic and now the high schooler would do everything possible to back up that claim.

"Any idea how to start this?" he asked. There didn't seem to be a switch nearby to turn the merry go round into moving.

"I don't know." Something drew her attention. And if she felt worry, there existed cause for alarm. "Look at this one." The lovely enchantress pointed at one of the figures on the ride. "It looks so real."

Admittedly, it looked real in the frightening way and not the this was a work of art variant. "It almost looks like..." Sam looked carefully at the face of the golden statue. Despite this being a Merry Go Round, a ride that represented happiness, this figure represented anything but.

"Are those... *Tears?*"

"They look so real." He answered. "I think we should leave." Sam said suddenly.

"Come on." She goaded. "You aren't scared of a statue, right?" Her wicked smile put his heart into sprint mode. Nothing but yes could be said to that face.

"We better figure out how to start..." he stopped short as the merry go round moved on its own. And the music sounded quite different. Carousels were supposed to be filled with goodness and the music, an exception. It played a music box tune like normal, but with one important issue. The sounds playing from the ride sounded...off.

Sam had never studied music before but recalled once in passing that music could change how it affected an audience with simply changing a few notes. Whatever that meant Sam could hear in play now. This waltz chilled him to the bone. The wind failed to leave an impression as a result.

"Get on." Samantha proved stronger than she looked as she snatched a dumbfounded teenage boy into the air and onto the carousel horse.

After a moment of sitting behind her, the emotionally distraught high schooler wished greatly to be in front. *Focus on her and not your stupid genetics!* He heard giggles in front. Despite the frightening music, she managed to keep a stable head.

"I watch stuff like this all the time. But being part of it is something else entirely." She afforded him privacy when the enchantress who continued to grab onto his heart tighter stared straight ahead.

"This is pretty amazing." He lied. In truth he wanted to get as far away from this place as possible. *I better get used to things like this. She's enjoying herself right now.* Realizing that he would have no choice but to be brave gave him some courage. This coincided perfectly with what Samantha said next.

"Do you know why I decided to give you a chance?" Now the lovely woman did turn around and look at him. "It is because you had the courage to treat me like a person instead of an object." She had flashed him many smiles tonight, and this one proved the most potent yet. Not because of teasing. Samantha spoke from the heart.

"You are truly a remarkable person Sam. Far braver than you know. You approached me and had the courage to ask me on a date. That's much more difficult than bringing me to a spooky place like this." Before she could continue heaping more praises on him, the ride stopped.

As the Merry Go Round moved to its resting place, Samuel stepped on board. "Time to go Sam." he uttered. "I have to kick you out now."

"Let's go." Sam looked to Samantha. The strange man's sudden appearance seemed to have shaken her seemingly indomitable spirit.

"Were you watching us?"

"Yes."

"You creep! I'm gonna call the police."

Sam moved to tell her to stop, but Samuel acted first.

"I own this property. If you call the police, you won't like what happens. In fact, I did not permit you in these grounds. Only your boyfriend."

The teenager flinched when described as such, preparing himself for a rejection. These two were not dating. This night simply a testing the waters situation. However, the next words out of the lovely enchantress' mouth filled him with joy to the point of tears.

"Please don't hurt him. We were just about to plan our next date." She had the chance to reject him right there but had affirmed how she felt to a stranger. A creepy one at that. Looming over them both, Sam noticed that Samuel had a crooked hooked nose. He looked like a villain from a cartoon show.

"You. Leave." He commanded and the teen ran away. He turned around to make sure that nothing horrible occurred behind. All he saw were two figures staring each other down on a carousel.

By the time he reached the parking lot and safety, the high schooler heaved, out of breath. The two had been in the park at least an hour and the sky far darker for it. Still, he would wait. Sam would be a terrible boyfriend if Samantha and he did not talk at least one more time.

He checked his phone again for the thousandth time. The night had ended, and with it a new day began. Sam pinched his cheeks to ensure he stood awake Samantha had not appeared in class all day. Indeed no one knew where she had gone.

Counting down to the ending bell, he vowed to get right in his car and return to the creepy carnival. He would have a word with Samuel. Fearing the worst, he considered calling the police beforehand. But his word against the man who owned the property made him reconsider.

Finally, after taking labored breaths the entire drive, Sam returned to where he had last seen his girlfriend. *Girlfriend* had an amazing ring to it. Of course, Sam would run that by her before it became official.

Samuel stood waiting for him at the gate. No surprises there "Did you return for her?"

"What did you do?!"

"Now now, no need to shout Sam." the calmness in the creepy man's voice confirmed that he should scream. "I will take you to her." Reluctantly, the high schooler complied.

"Where is she!?" He screeched. This courage came from her. Whatever had happened, Sam would fix this right here and now.

"Look closely." Hook nose pointed the way. The carousel looked a bit different from before. In the daylight, Sam noticed something. There were pieces missing. The ride did not have perfect symmetry. But a new figurine stood on the ride. And he certainly would have noticed its presence last night.

Scared to look, the high schooler crept nearer. The closer he reached, the worse his imagination became. Finally, he dashed like a madman. And found his beloved Samantha. A look of horror transfixed on her face. Forever held in that gaze.

"Before you ask to let her go, don't bother. She's part of the ride now." Samuel raised his arms to the sky. "Samantha is truly a girl of beauty. And now that beauty forevermore will be part of this attraction.

Sam fell to the ground, equal parts hissing combined with open sobbing. "Why..." He whispered. "Why would you do this? Why would you kill an innocent teenager?"

"She's alive." Samuel spoke with such intense seriousness that the high schooler wanted to stand up and break his face open. "In fact, Samantha achieved immortality! Complete. Unlike you. I chose her because she is a creature of perfection. You however are empty. Devoid of purpose. Now get out of my sight filth!"

The teen ran away because he didn't know what to do. He had lost the first woman to ever profess her love. The first woman to call him brave. And now he lacked the courage to avenge her death.

Sam fled from that place, leaving all the happiness and courage he gained the night before in that cursed carnival, never to be reclaimed.

About the Author

Ross Ellison is an Author, Entertainer, Video Game Streamer, and All Around Menace to Society. Living in Orlando, Florida he currently is working on the next two novels in his Search For Eden Series which the End of Utopia Anthology serves as an introduction for. He also is working on a Post Apocalyptic Series with the working title of "Earth Everafter"

University of Central Florida's Online Publication Imprint selected his work for publication . He works at an online publication called BentoByte where one can find reviews on Anime and Video Games as well as articles on pop culture. Ross pesters society at large with his political commentary.

Writers of Central Florida or Thereabouts selected Ross as a featured Speaker. He is known as "the writer who always goes first" at the many open mics hosted by the organization. Odyssey Orlando has also published multiple pieces of work by Ross.

Whether through his Dark Fantasy Fiction, or commentary on issues that strike his fancy, Ross strives to entertain and educate audiences. Though his writing may deal with difficult issues, these are the ideas which drive society forward. Braving through his work will reward readers with high entertainment value as well as the potential for learning.

He is always looking for collaborators to aid in his endeavors of bringing his work to life. If you are interested in working with him, or have an idea to pitch, do not hesitate to visit the Collaborations Page

DEAD MAN'S CARNIVAL

Valerie Puri

The pier in St. Petersburg, Florida was finally reopening. Mitch had lost track of how many years it'd been since the city demolished the old one. Originally, the plan was to replace it with an ugly, space-age type monstrosity, but the community spoke up and shot that down; the new design was timeless

Today was the grand opening and, to celebrate, the city set up a carnival. Mitch wasn't big into carnivals - the rides always made him sick - but his best friend Joe begged him to come along.

"Come on... It's free, the city's paying for it. You don't even have to shell out anything unless you get hungry or something."

"All right," Mitch relented, "but you're driving."

They had to park several blocks away, and by the time they got to the carnival, his feet were killing him.

Joe shook his shoulder. "Check it out! They built a roller coaster around the building in the middle."

The thing was massive, with smaller rides and carnival games surrounding the coaster. It was pretty impressive they could pull it off. But, walking under the rickety thing to get to the building, didn't appeal to Mitch.

"Let's go see what's at the back, it's too crowded up here," Mitch suggested.

They passed a fire-eater with cropped red hair who blew a flame so close to Mitch, he worried his eyebrows would get singed. She blew a smokey kiss at him and winked, making his cheeks grow hot. She's cute, he thought, imagining that kissing her would taste the way a campfire smelled.

"Look what I have," Joe said, pulling an apple juice bottle from one of the larger pockets of his cargo pants.

"Why'd you bother sneaking in juice?"

"It's not juice, it's tequila," Joe laughed. "We can get sloshed tonight."

He unscrewed the cap, took a swig, and offered the bottle to Mitch.

He wasn't into tequila, but when you were twenty and couldn't buy alcohol yourself, you took what you could get.

Swallowing a gulp, he immediately regretted it. It burned the back of his throat so bad he felt he could breathe fire like the cute performer.

"How about we go in there?" Joe asked, pointing to a clown fun house.

It was creepy as hell. The entrance was through the mouth of a clown that looked like it came straight out of a Stephen King novel.

"I'm not going in that train wreck."

"How about a shipwreck instead?" Joe asked.

Behind the clown house, was a pirate ship tethered to the pier. It looked like it'd been around for a couple hundred years, at least. Its hull was crusted in barnacles, the wood dull and rotted. All that was left of the sails were gray tattered rags flapping in the wind.

"Okay, that's pretty cool. How do you think they made it look so real?" Mitch asked.

"Who cares? Let's go see what they did inside."

When they got closer, Joe pointed to the front of the ship.

"Check out the boobs on that mermaid."

The carved half-fish, half-woman on the bow was tinged with decay.

"Rotten wooden boobs? Man, you're weird.

"Rotten boobs, rotten boobs," a screeching voice called out.

A bird perched beside the plank leading onto the ship squawked and spoke again.

"Rotten boobs."

"It's a freaking parrot," Joe laughed, taking another drink. "Hey, you think he likes tequila?"

"Aw, man. Don't give it alcohol. That's not cool."

It squawked again.

"Tequila. Tequila."

"See? It's practically begging for a drink."

Joe poured some into the cap and held it out.

The parrot scooted closer to Joe's hand. It opened its beak and lapped up the tequila, and when the cap was empty, it bobbed its head up and down.

"Tequila."

"What's your name, bird?" Joe asked.

"Gaspar."

"Works for me," Joe shrugged. "You want some more, Gaspar?"

The bird bobbed up and down again.

Joe flashed Mitch a grin as if to say I told you so, the bird loves tequila.

Mitch pursed his lips. "Come on, let's go explore this pirate ship fun house."

He took the bottle from Joe, putting it to his lips before he could pour more for the bird. He gave it back and climbed the plank.

It was a rickety old board without any handrails - which was surprising given safety standards. One misstep and someone could easily fall into the water below.

Mitch hopped from the plank onto the ship deck, the faded boards creaking in protest. He didn't see anyone else on the ship.

Odd, he thought. Maybe everyone is still working their way to the back of the pier.

Craning his head, he looked up the main mast with its crow's nest near the top. The alcohol was already kicking in, making his head swim.

Joe shoved past him, jogging to the back of the ship. He ran up the steps to the helm and grabbed the wheel.

"Hey Mitch, take a picture of me being the captain," he called out.

Gaspar flew to Joe and perched on his shoulder.

"Captain Joe. Captain Joe," the bird said.

"Uh, how did it know your name?" Mitch asked.

"What? I don't know. Just take the picture before it flies away. This is awesome."

Mitch pulled out his phone and took the photo.

"Done."

"Cool. Tweet it out and tag me. Hashtag pirate ship," Joe laughed.

Mitch opened Twitter on his smartphone, but it wouldn't load. He checked his signal strength. Nothing.

"I can't get a connection. Maybe the new pier doesn't have good cell signal."

"Eh, tweet it later."

DEMONIC CARNIVAL

Mitch opened the door beneath the helm and stepped inside, finding a richly decorated room.

On his right was a dining table set with silver dishes and massive candelabras. To the left a plush bed was tucked in the corner of the room. At the far end were massive windows looking out over the water. In front of him was a desk with a map spread out on it.

Curious, Mitch examined the old and tattered map. Land bordered the outside of the map with a large body of water in the middle.

"The Great Bay of Mexico?" Mitch read aloud.

"It's the Gulf of Mexico, get it right," Joe said from behind him.

"Tell that to the map," Mitch pointed to the tabletop. "You know, for a fun house, this place is kind of boring."

"Nah, you just need to let loose a little. See, look here. A captain's outfit."

Joe took a dusty outfit from a peg on the wall, pulling on the coat and placing the wide brimmed hat on his head.

Mitch sniggered. Joe could have stepped right out of a cheesy pirate movie.

"You look like a Captain Hook reject."

"Maybe, but at least I look like a captain." Joe puffed out his chest and struck his best Captain Morgan pose.

"Okay, that's freaky. You look just like the guy in the picture behind you."

Joe turned and scrunched his face to study the painting.

"I'm way more handsome than this dude." Joe pointed to a painting next to the one he'd been studying. "This one looks kind of like you."

Mitch walked over to take a closer look.

Mitch's nose had a twist from when he broke it a few years ago; the young man in the painting did too. He also had the same messy hair and brown eyes. Everything was the same except the clothes - the man in the portrait wore something from the seventeen hundreds.

"It's got to be some sort of trick mirror," Mitch said.

He waved his hand in front of the painting and swayed from side to side. The portrait didn't move.

"Nope. Not a mirror."

"Maybe they have cameras and just printed out a picture of us when we got here," Joe said, scratching at his portrait with a fingernail. Old paint flaked off. "I don't know, this is kind of weird."

"And not fun," Mitch added.

"Let's see what else there is to do on this ship and then go ride the roller coaster."

Mitch didn't care to go on any rides, but he could talk to the cute fire-eater instead.

"Yeah, let's do that."

When they left the cabin, the air was frigid. A mist had settled around the ship obscuring their visibility. Mitch could just make out the outline of the pier and the colorful lights through the mist, the chaotic drone of the carnival carrying on faintly in the background.

"Fog ahead," the parrot announced from the helm.

"Wow, they went all out with fog machines and everything," Joe said. "Let's see what's down below."

The parrot found its perch on Joe's shoulder, who offered Gaspar another capful of tequila, which it rapidly drank.

The stairs creaked as they descended below deck. As if on cue, oil lanterns burst to life, bathing the open space in light. They swung on their hooks as the ship began rocking back and forth.

"What the -?"

Joe stumbled back into Mitch, Gaspar flapping his wings to remain on Joe's shoulder

"Hey, watch it!"

"I was not expecting that," Joe laughed. "They have a fake skeleton just hanging out over here."

The skeleton was dressed in a tattered cream shirt, brown trousers, and rough leather boots. The bones were aged and porous. Its hand gripped a glass bottle the worn label read: tequila.

"It looks so real," Mitch marveled.

"Look at that. Even the pirate skeleton appreciates a good drink," Joe said, raising the apple juice bottle in a mock toast to the bones.

Gaspar bobbed up and down in excitement.

"Cheers! Cheers!" The bird squawked.

Mitch and Joe moved further into the ship's hold. More skeletons were staged as if they were sleeping in hammocks, sinewy muscles clinging to the bones.

Joe poked a muscle on one of the sleeping skeletons.

"Whoever their prop guy is, he's good. It feels real, kinda like beef jerky."

From the other side of the hammocks, something glinted in the lantern light.

"Woah, he's really good. Check out that chest of gold."

DEMONIC CARNIVAL

Mitch rushed over to a wooden box, gold coins spilling from a hole onto the floor. Crouching beside it, he raised the lid.

"Wow," he gasped.

He plunged his fingers into the contents. Treasure overflowed from his cupped hands as he lifted them the gold coins heavier than he expected. They didn't seem like the cheap, plastic stuff from a party store.

"Imagine if this was real. We would be rich," Mitch said.

"Ho, ho, check this out!" Joe pulled a sword from a nearby barrel and lunged at the air, dueling an invisible foe. "My pirate captain outfit is complete."

"Wake up," Gaspar squawked. "Wake up for the captain."

Mitch raised his eyebrows.

"What's that supposed to mean?"

"No idea." Joe shrugged, causing the parrot to flap its wings to keep balance on his shoulder.

The ship creaked and something stirred in the hammocks.

"Holy crap!" Mitch shrieked.

He lost his balance and fell, gold flying from his hands, clattering to the floor. He scrambled away, until his back pressed against the side of the ship.

A gold coin rolled across the floor toward the hammocks, striking a boot and toppling over. A bony hand covered in mottled grey flesh reached down and picked it up. The owner of the hand raised the shiny metal until it was at eye level. Greenish flesh pulled away from blackened teeth in a gruesome smile.

Every hammock was empty. The skeleton occupants stood, watching, waiting. They had more muscle and flesh than Mitch remembered, more man than skeleton now. It was as if time were reversing. Instead of decomposing, they were... recomposing.

"This... this..." Mitch stammered. "This is real?"

"Ready the crew. Ready the sails," the parrot ordered.

The pirate corpses shambled in different directions. Some went down to the lower hold, others climbed the stairs to the deck above.

Mitch crawled over to Joe, trying to stay as small as possible. He didn't want to draw any more of the dead's attention. He stood on shaky legs when he rejoined his friend.

Joe wore a lopsided grin.

"Are you as freaked out as I am?" Mitch shrilled.

The corpse near the stairs rose from his seat. He raised the old glass bottle of tequila to Joe and brought the rim to his cracked lips.

"Nothing to fear, Mitch. He's just returning my toast."

Mitch's jaw dropped. How could his friend be so calm when the skeletons regrew flesh and rose from the dead?

"And the others?" Mitch asked. "What about them?"

"You're right. Let's go check on the crew."

Joe sheathed his new sword. He snatched a silver goblet from a nearby table before he strode up the stairs.

Mitch glanced over his shoulder. He didn't want to be left down there alone with any corpses. He ran after Joe, taking the steps two at a time. When he emerged onto the main deck, the ship had transformed. Instead of rotting wood and rags for sails, it all looked brand new.

The wood was a deep brown, polished to a high shine. Massive white sails billowed in the wind. A corpse in the crow's nest raised the Jolly Roger flag.

There was no trace of the pier or anything that resembled Tampa Bay. They were sailing down Florida's unsettled coastline.

"How is this possible?" Mitch asked.

"Why question it, when we can enjoy it? Look at me, I'm the new captain and you'll be my first mate."

"Captain for the crew," Gaspar said.

"Gaspar, what year is it?" Joe asked the parrot.

"Seventeen eighteen," the bird answered.

"See Mitch? Just relax, they won't hurt us. Let's enjoy sailing the high seas during the heyday of the pirate trade."

Mitch frowned, following Joe up the steps to the helm of the ship.

Joe poured the tequila into his silver goblet and tossed the empty apple juice bottle over the side of the ship.

"Ahoy you scurvy dogs!" Joe shouted to the crew below.

Mitch covered his face with his hand. "You look and sound like a walking stereotype."

"At least I look good," Joe winked.

"I never said...," Mitch sighed, "never mind."

Joe raised his goblet to the crew and took a drink.

"Are you ready to plunder the seas for treasure and tequila?"

"Arrrr," the corpses shouted.

"Your plan is to raid islands for liquor?" Mitch asked.

"Yeah. Check out my crew, a bunch of walking corpses. I always wondered what zombies would be like drunk."

Mitch rolled his eyes. "Whatever, Joe. As long as I can be back home by dinner."

"You there!" Joe pointed to a corpse with a peg leg.

"Set a course for Mexico and take the helm."

"Mmm," it said.

The corpse's wooden leg thumped on the deck as it approached.

"Why Mexico?"

"Mitch, you really need to lighten up. Live on the edge for once. How often will we get to captain a time traveling pirate ship filled with zombies?"

Mitch gaped at his friend.

"Before today, I would have said never."

"Exactly. So embrace the adventure. What do they make in Mexico?"

Mitch shrugged. "Really good tacos?"

Joe grinned at him. "And tequila."

Peg Leg finally hobbled up the stairs to the helm. Joe stood aside and let him take the wheel. The zombie stared ahead with cloudy eyes.

"Set course, set course," Gaspar squawked.

The zombie grunted in acknowledgement.

"I'll be in my cabin," Joe announced to his undead crew.

He strode down the stairs, with Mitch on his heels.

"Think about it Joe, if we really did travel back in time, wouldn't raiding Mexico for alcohol screw up history?"

Joe laughed as he threw open the door to the captain's quarters, plopping down on the bed and reclining against the pillows.

"Seizing a couple barrels of tequila from some small port town won't destroy the world as we know it."

"But what about the space time continuum?" Mitch asked.

"What about it?"

"I don't know, we'll break it somehow. If we really are in the past, we shouldn't do anything that could change the future," he paced the floor, trying to figure things out.

"Unless we were supposed to do the thing in the past to ensure the future as we know it would happen as it should."

Mitch stopped pacing, his head spinning. How did all time travel stuff work anyway? He wasn't even sure if this was real. It was all a dream - it had to be. That was the only thing that made sense. He pinched his arm to see if it hurt; it did.

"You're not dreaming, Mitch. This is real. Take a look at those portraits again... they are us."

The paintings in the room no longer had old paint flaking off - they were pristine and clear as day. It was like looking in a mirror. The longer Mitch looked, the more he realized Joe was right. They'd somehow got sucked into this mess of a zombie pirate ship, their portraits hanging on the wall of the captain's cabin.

The ship jerked to a halt, sending Mitch crashing to the ground. He picked himself up and rubbed his elbow.

"What happened?"

Joe rose from the bed and strode out of the room.

"Alright men, get ready to plunder," he shouted from the deck.

Wondering what on earth his friend could mean, he joined him outside. The pirate ship was anchored off the coast near a small, crude town, with boats tethered to wooden docks. A group of corpse-pirates was already rowing to shore in a small boat.

"Where are we?" Mitch scratched his head.

"Mexico. Mexico," Gaspar answered.

"How did we get here from Florida so fast?"

Joe laughed. "Do you have to question everything? I would guess that the time traveling pirate ship can also sail at warp speed."

Joe put his arm around Mitch and pulled him close gesturing to the horizon as if painting a picture.

"Imagine, people will be telling tales of us for hundreds of years. What if we are the ghost ship in all the stories we only heard about. What if that town there will spread tales of the undead sailors for generations. We are making history by planting the seeds of legend."

Screams erupted from the shore as the zombie crew raided homes for treasure and drink. Mitch watched as they rowed back to the ship with their plunder. When the crew rejoined the ship with their haul, Joe examined the goods.

The zombies brought back silver platters and cups, gold and jewelry, and a few crates filled with tequila bottles. Joe took a bottle, opened it, and smelled it.

"That's the good stuff," he said, pouring himself a drink.

"Well done, crew. To celebrate, everyone grab a bottle and drink it all."

The corpses shuffled forward, each taking a bottle of tequila. Some even took two. They drank the contents as if it were water.

"Peg Leg, take us back home," Joe said

The corpse with the wooden leg took the helm and turned the ship around into a blanket of fog.

Mitch and Joe leaned back against the door to the captain's cabin, watching the zombie crew stumble into each other and topple over. The corpses exchanged a series of incoherent "arrs" and "urgs" when they collided.

"You should ask her out, you know." Joe said.

"Who?"

"The fire breathing girl. She's into you."

Mitch felt his cheeks flush. She was pretty and seemed like a lot of fun; she ate fire for a living, after all.

He smiled as he watched the drunk corpses aimlessly roam the deck of the ship.

"Yeah, I think I will."

The skin on the zombies began to slough off as they decayed. Their muscles shriveled until there was hardly anything left clinging to their bones.

"Time for bed," the parrot said.

Gaspar flew to the helm and perched on the wheel.

The skeletons shuffled below deck. The ship itself lost its sheen and the wood creaked as it dried out, like the bones of the dead.

"We must be moving forward through time," Joe said.

The fog around them evaporated, revealing the bright lights and sounds of the carnival. They were back at the pier. Joe returned his jacket and hat to the captain's quarters, pointing to the sunset.

"There, you see? I got you back before dinner."

Mitch laughed. After witnessing skeletons rise from the dead, traveling through time on a ghost ship, and zombies getting drunk off tequila, being home in time for dinner seemed trivial.

They replaced the plank and walked over it to return to the pier. It felt good to stand on solid ground again. A couple guys passed them and boarded the pirate ship. Mitch overhead them mention how it looked so real. He chuckled to himself. If only they knew.

Mitch scanned the crowd until he saw the fire-eater. There she was, cute as ever with her short purple hair. He could have sworn her hair had been red, but it might have been the lighting. She blew a large flame in the air to the joy of the nearby crowd.

He walked through the people and approached her.

"Would you like to grab a bite to eat?"

She gave him a dazzling smile that made his cheeks grow hot.

"Sure. I have a break in fifteen minutes. Meet me at the corn dog stand."

Mitch beamed at her. "I'll be there."

He glanced over his shoulder back at the pirate ship. It was cloaked in fog and fading away. He wondered how the two newcomers would handle the zombie pirates. Sometimes you had to take a page out of Joe's book and just roll with it. Otherwise you might become a zombie yourself.

ABOUT THE AUTHOR

Valerie Puri is an author of Paranormal, Fantasy, and Young Adult. As a writer of both short stories and novels, she enjoys the flexibility of writing tales of any length. Her favorite aspect of writing is the ability to create something out of nothing. She loves building worlds readers can visualize and filling those worlds with complex characters and storylines. Valerie believes that the experiences we have in life are just stories waiting to be written.

In 2016, she published her debut novel, The Crimson Tree, a thrilling paranormal tale inspired by true events. The main source of inspiration for this story was a number of experiences her sister encountered in her home. She went on to publish The Dociles, book one of The Secret Archives Trilogy, her young adult dystopian series. Valerie's work can be found in anthologies such as Demonic Anthologies, Thrill of the Hunt, and We Know the Truth, Do You? Readers can look forward to future novels and short stories with paranormal and urban fantasy aspects in the near future, including a trilogy she is co-authoring in the Dark Projects world.

When she's not writing, she enjoys spending time with her family, traveling, or listening to audio books. She is a Florida transplant, but part of her will always call the Midwest home.

Website:
www.valeriepuri.com

Instagram:
@AuthorValeriePuri

Goodreads:
www.goodreads.com/
valeriepuri

Facebook:
@AuthorValeriePuri

Twitter:
@ValeriePuri

BookBub:
www.bookbub.com/
authors/valerie-puri

Facebook Group:
www.facebook.com/
groups/puripals

Amazon:
www.amazon.com/
author/valeriepuri

THE SEVENTH TIME IS WORTH A TRY

Teresa Edmond-Sargeant

Jasmine loved seeing the different faces around her as she jogged on the sidewalk in the city's central park. She relished in getting back into her morning workout routine after settling into her new home in a new city, six months after leaving behind the madness that was her relationship.

Rising above the green, further in the back of the park, were familiar sights of a carnival — roller coaster tracks, a Ferris wheel, and signs and banners advertising traditional carnival fare such as "Funnel Cakes," "Cotton Candy," and "Lemonade." Jasmine did hear about a local club organizing the carnival as a fundraiser. She made a mental note about checking the event out.

Jasmine turned a corner on the concrete path, deciding to take a route in the park she had not taken yet. She tripped over a broken branch. Instead of collapsing onto the grass, a hole opened up in front of her.

Her jaw dropped as she gawked at the expanse below. "What is this?" she questioned, and pondered about why something that looked like a sinkhole would materialize at her feet. As well, she considered whether moving to this new city was such a bright idea in light of the personal misery she endured in her old hometown.

DEMONIC CARNIVAL

But before she could step back from the monstrous hole, she slipped and fell into it. Time passed her as she floated downward through this bottomless pit. At last her feet touched the ground but still, nothing but blackness surrounded her.

What's happening? she asked herself.

Her nerves shook throughout her body. She placed her hands against the blackness, hoping to touch a wall and discover something resembling an exit. No sign of any door appeared — not a crack through which light could shine, not a doorway or window frame, not a doorknob thrusting out indicating a door's presence.

Then from out of the void, lucite bottles populated shelf after shelf, making the surrounding seem more like a quirky boutique than wherever she ended up. Each bottle glowed with a different, singular color that together, covered a rainbow's worth of hues – enough illumination to brighten the dark void. The bottles' small, medium, and large shapes ranged from more conventional types like cubes and rectangles to more eclectic fare such as a miniature skyscraper, a dog, and a cat. Jasmine looked across the void to the other side, where more lucite bottles lined the shelves. She walked past the shelves and about three yards down the void, where she discovered an aluminum boat with three benches in it, floating in the blackness. A pair of oars lied inside it. Its silver color stood out against the darkness.

She approached a shelf closest to her, peered inside one of them, then picked it up for further examination. In this bottle, a man and a woman embraced in a slow dance on a floor at what appeared to be a party. She wore a black cocktail with her hair styled. Her partner had on a sports jacket, slacks, and a tie. Jasmine recognized them as both herself and the man.

"Oh no!" Jasmine said. "All this can't be at the hands of –"

She dropped the bottle, but before it hit the ground, the bottle flew up and placed itself in its space on the shelf.

"Our date on our first anniversary," a voice said from behind her. "When we went to that hospital gala celebrating their 100th anniversary. Everybody that was anybody was there – and I made sure that night, they knew I had someone like you under my arms, someone who could further emphasize how much of a great guy I am."

Jasmine turned around to see a tall man, a man whose appearance once possessed an off-kilter adorable charm but now, in the six months since they broke up, struck her as nothing more than conventional plainness. What was once a head full of vibrant redness was now thinning with greying temples. Gone was the healthy hue of blush from his complexion; now a relative paleness washed over it. His once well-defined jaw now looked oversized. The nose that Jasmine once believed to be boyishly quaint now bulged with ruddiness.

Furthermore, Jasmine was amazed that the love she once had for this man blinded her to how out-of-shape he has been. His white t-shirt draped over his shapeless chest and covered a stomach so huge one could wonder if he swallowed Pluto. His blue and yellow bermuda shorts hit his knees while red hair covered his shins and calves. He donned sandals on his disproportionately huge feet. In spite of what Jasmine now noticed were all his physical shortcomings, his hazel eyes stood out as the lone attractive feature, even up to now. Alas, his other features buried the eyes' attractiveness.

"Xavier?" Jasmine asked.

"Welcome to our tunnel of love, Jasmine," Xavier said, gesturing at the dimly lit setting around him. "A tribute, a shrine, a testament to the two years of our perfect, undying love and how it should be a model for all romantic relationships between you and me, about how no matter how different you and I are – how different your kind and my kind are – we had quite a loving relationship."

Jasmine looked around herself in flippant disbelief. "So this place here, this tunnel of love ... you choose to locate it underneath a city park?"

Xavier stepped up to a shelf of lucite bottles and lifted one vessel. "It's transferrable – it goes where I go as well as where I want it to go."

Jasmine eyed the bottle's contents. The moving image showed one of the several times she and Xavier sipped coffee on a pavilion outside a café.

Jasmine glared at Xavier. "How did you find me? I told you not to contact me anymore. That's why I moved out of my hometown and to another city: to make sure of that. You may be a supernatural being with supernatural powers, but we both know your knowledge of humans is limited to the 24-hour news cycle, best-selling pop psychology books, and Facebook. I want nothing to do with you, understand? You've violated my boundaries – to use the words you so love to use whenever you spoke constantly about your therapy. By the way, why therapy? I thought your kind didn't need to be psychoanalyzed in order to get better."

Xavier put the lucite bottle with the café memory back on its spot on the shelf. "Don't you understand how much therapy I needed so I can move on from you? I was a mess since you dumped me. Vulnerability is something I didn't expect to feel when I got involved with you. When I went searching for love, I couldn't find it with anyone else of my kind, let alone my family. Even my mother – a goddess of love – couldn't show me because she let her marriage to my father corrupt her. I couldn't find love with an angel or some other good supernatural being because it's just too complicated. So I figured the next best thing to find love is to get in a relationship with a human." He paused. "Hence, you. And in pursuit of that love, I started mimicking other human characteristics too – the desire for love came with a desire for attention, and then a desire to leave my legacy on this earth – you understand.

Disgust crossed Jasmine's face. "Really? You mimicking human characteristics? Let me tell you that in hindsight, when we were together, that mask of yours slipped off once in a while and revealed your true nature. I was so blinded by love, I ignored them and yet in the back of my head couldn't help but wonder why you'd say those things. But now, seeing all this around me, it makes sense."

Xavier contorted his face in surprise. "Like when?"

"Like that one time you threatened to uproot my nails and gouge my eyes out because I over-tipped a waiter at a restaurant on one of our dates. Or telling me you'd have me drawn and quartered because I splurged too much on discounted air freshener at some big box store. Or how sometimes at parties, I'd overhear you say something about yourself that no human would ever say. One time you told a mayor that you begged the Roman emperor Nero to hire you as a political advisor and his refusal to do so led to his inevitable downfall," Jasmine said. "Another time, you lamented to the president of a cancer awareness nonprofit that some pope in medieval times never credited you for his rise to power."

"So once in a while I let slip of my true nature," Xavier said, shrugging. "I mean, why spend all that money on air freshener when it's better to save up for a getaway trip to Punta Cana? But in getting back to my point: can't you see I missed you? There's no other way for me to elaborate on that other than by creating an underground hallmark celebrating the two years our relationship lasted. This is also a good time to tell you I've written a book about those years. It's going on sale next month on Amazon."

Jasmine scowled. "You wrote a book about us?"

"Yes – but only nice things!" Xavier said, holding his hands up. "I'm grateful for the time we shared together. It's called 'Bearings of My Soul: How One Woman Made Me Human.' Since I'm the only one of my kind that has been the first to be in a relationship with a human, I feel that kind of makes me an expert. So that means I have something to contribute to humankind."

Jasmine scrunched her face in disgust. She checked the walls with her eyes for any cracks or other opening she might find as a sign of escape – and hope. "Somebody get me out of here!"

"This is about mending fences," Xavier said, ignoring Jasmine's scream. His tone was low with a hint of pouting. "Don't you want to mend fences, like good exes should? Let bygones be bygones?"

"And to think I ever got involved with someone like you – a demon!" Jasmine said. "When you first approached me at Dave's house for his campaign launch party, I loved how unassuming you were in your actions yet confident in your intelligence when we conversed about the locals. You didn't try hitting on me at all. Yet the last two years was all a charade for you, using me and exploiting me for your own selfish end. You really hurt me – a demon to the core."

Xavier looked down the tunnel, where a framed portrait had appeared. It hung on the wall of the void – or hovered in the air, Jasmine couldn't really tell. The portrait was of herself dressed in a white ballroom gown, posing next to a short pillar with her arm propped on it and a tiara on her head. Jasmine looked down at her sweatshirt and sweatpants and caressed her ponytail – a sharp contrast from her appearance in the portrait.

"Dave was a good friend of yours and mine too," Xavier said. "The first time we met at his place ... what can I say? Your beauty struck me, so I wanted to get to know you better."

Jasmine studied her portrait, frowned at Xavier and crossed her arms. "This is why we broke up. This, right here, is what you do."

"What do I do?"

Jasmine sighed and continued, enduring the drudgery that goes into explaining her emotions to a demon. "You don't respect my wishes to be left alone, you bully and harass me with your blowhard arrogance, and then when you get called out on it, you sit back and moan like you're the victim. Then again, you are a demon, so all that is pretty much in your nature."

Xavier shook his head. "It's not being a victim if you understand your own boundaries and speak up for what you want. Understand, I did everything I did because I have to keep a beautiful woman like you with me. How else would you date me?"

Jasmine recognized the sappy sliminess in his voice again. Fed up with Xavier's machinations, she ran toward the shelves of lucite bottles. One by one, she grabbed each off the shelf and threw them on the ground. Yet all these bottles returned to their rightful places, each memory within the container intact, and each memory illuminating with more intensified colors.

Noticing the oars inside the boat, Jasmine ran over and seized one of them. With it, she swung at the bottles, knocking them off the shelves then attacked the shelves. Yet the shelves did not break, and as soon as the bottles made close contact with the ground, they all returned to their rightful spots. All throughout Jasmine's destruction, Xavier had stood with his hands behind his back.

"Get me out of here! Get me out!" Jasmine screamed during her rampage.

Noticing that her efforts didn't damage let alone destroy anything, fury flamed up within Jasmine. She charged at Xavier, aiming the oar at him like a lance. "If you don't get me out of here, I swear I'll —"

Unwavered by Jasmine's menace, Xavier snapped his fingers. The oar vanished from Jasmine's hands and she found her body, wrists, and ankles bound up in chains and a gag in her mouth, lying on the ground.

Xavier crowded in on Jasmine's personal space. Her heart pounded against the inside of her chest. Her forehead got hot. She was close to sweating.

"Let's go on a trip, shall we?" Xavier asked, his breath warming on Jasmine's face. She recalled tossing out garbage that smelled better than his breath.

Waving his finger, Xavier raised the bounded Jasmine up into the air and lowered her into the boat. He stepped into the transportation. Jasmine struggled at first to break out of the chains, but gave up and remained in her spot. She noticed that her portrait had disappeared. With one oar, Xavier paddled the boat down the tunnel in the void, passing shelf after shelf, and lucite bottle after lucite bottle displaying memories from their relationship.

"You have no idea what it's like to be the son of a goddess of love and a demon," Xavier said as they sailed along, crying and sniffing. "You have no idea what it's like to struggle with a lifelong identity crisis, to find my way in the underworld, to–"

Jasmine had heard Xavier's lament about his family so many times in the relationship, she practically committed it to memory word for word. After his ranting, Xavier calmed down. His loud breathing echoed through the tunnel as he kept rowing. He continued to weep in silence over the misery of his supernatural life, though how much more silence could there be in this quiet void? From listening to Xavier's sobs, Jasmine sighed. Being in a relationship with him had drained her. To be trapped in a void with him and hear him cry in self-pity was too much.

After what seemed to be an eternity, the boat stopped sailing. Xavier navigated it to his right as if he were pulling up to a bank, though nothing was there. Toward what may be the end of the tunnel, something glittered from the top of a column, an indication that it could be the highlight of this strange exhibit. Xavier stepped out of the boat. With a snap of his fingers, the chains and gag in Jasmine's mouth disappeared. She stepped out of the boat and together, the two made their way past the shelves of lucite bottles toward the display. Jasmine approached the glittering item, and it became clear to her: a diamond engagement ring. She reeled.

"No," she said, shaking her head. "No, no, no, no, no!"

Xavier nodded. "Yes, yes, yes. The engagement ring I gave you when I proposed, right before you abandoned me to care for your mother."

"I did not abandon you! My mother needed me – she was sick and dying! I said I'd be back in a few weeks or so, and I did come back. And while I was in Boston, I kept in touch!"

"Sure you kept in touch, and sure you returned ... after the funeral five weeks later. You may have not said along the lines of 'I'm breaking up with you,' but you implied that by going to Boston. By the way, how is your mother? Still dead, I assume?" Xavier's voice, when he asked his question, had no trace of sarcasm or irony whatsoever.

Though Xavier's question had more of a lack of self-awareness than a malicious tone, Jasmine raised a fist to Xavier to punch him, but he held up a finger. "Not unless you want to get chained up again," he said. Reluctance seeped into Jasmine's body, and she lowered her fist.

"She was fifty-eight when she died, right?" Xavier asked. "I'm sure being that she had stage 4 breast cancer, doctors couldn't have done much to save her anyway. So your flying out to Boston wasn't going to make a difference."

Jasmine's eyes stung with tears. "Take that back."

Xavier circled Jasmine. Each footstep echoed throughout the otherwise silent void.

"Although you dumped me, I had it in my heart to take you back 24 hours later after your begging and pleading," Xavier said.

"You were the one who dumped me for the seventh time! When you called me to propose a second time, I said no because I was fed up with the makeup and breakup cycle of our relationship."

"You know what they say: the seventh time is worth a try," Xavier said, smiling the same goofy, toothy smile that was his trademark in the memories the bottles contained.

"Nobody says that!" Jasmine said. She seized the ring off the display, threw it into the void, and watched it disappear. "Propose with that!"

Xavier gawked at the spot where the ring disappeared into and turned to Jasmine. "That was an evil thing you did, to desecrate our love like that. To desecrate it at all! I created this tunnel of love for you – for us! I wrote a book on us!" Xavier seethed. Air exhausted from his flaring nostrils. "If I can't have you, no one can. You must be punished for ever defying me."

Xavier shook wildly like a bucking horse at a rodeo. Jasmine backed away from him, unsure if he'd explode or keel over dead. His torso expanded, ripping through his t-shirt and Bermuda shorts. More red hair sprouted and grew thicker on his torso, as well as his face, neck, arms and legs. Fangs cut through his mouth and grew until the end of his chin, and he grew from around six feet to eight feet. Yet certain facets of his appearance remained: his chest was still so flat he appeared as if he practically had none, and he still retained his rotund stomach. Yet underneath the fur, the fangs and his overall inhumane hideousness, his hazel eyes retained their shape and their charm. To Jasmine, Xavier in his demon form looked nothing more than like a redheaded Yeti, an appearance that chilled her skin from head to toe, wrenched her stomach, and sped up her breathing.

Xavier exposed his sharpened teeth, stretched his jaw to his chest like a snake about to consume his prey, and unleashed his ungodly breath on Jasmine. She reclined, avoiding the stench. She reached for the lone oar nearby, swung it at Xavier's head, and hit him. Xavier fell over. Jasmine smashed the oar into the blackness to break it in half. She then drove a splintered tip of one of the pieces into Xavier's chest. Black blood oozed from the injury. He looked at the wood protruding from his chest and screamed. Jasmine scurried away from him. He crawled toward her while gasping for air. He grasped at her feet, but she stepped back from him.

"Why would you do this to me, after all we've had?" he asked. Tears streamed from his hazel eyes. "You have no idea what it's like to be the son of a goddess of love and a demon. You have no idea –"

"'What it's like to struggle with a lifelong identity, to find my way in the underworld –'" Jasmine interrupted. "I know – I've only heard this story, like, twenty-five-thousand times!"

The void quaked around Jasmine, causing the shelved memory bottles to shake. Jasmine clasped the back of her head, squatted, and curled up into a ball as debris fell around her. The rumbling rattled her nerves. She inhaled and exhaled to calm herself but to no avail.

Jasmine didn't know how long the "tunnel of love's" self-destruction lasted. All she remembered was a lucite bottle rolled toward her and at her feet. She snatched it up and got a glimpse inside it: their slow dancing on their first anniversary date at the 100th anniversary hospital gala. When she uncurled herself and stood up, the void around her disappeared, replaced by a more familiar environment: trees populating the grounds, pavement underneath her feet, and the lamppost-lined sidewalk only some distance from her. Park dwellers continued with their activities – jogging, dog walking, biking, and so forth -- as if no one noticed a hole open up in the ground.

Though happiness filled Jasmine at the thought of having escaped the anguish her ex just put her through, she lost her motive to jog. A shame, she thought, for she had another three miles of her daily five to run. Instead, she basked in the sun's brightness drenching her with relief from the void, wanting to put Xavier and his "tunnel of love" behind her.

The skyline of carnival rides in the park got Jasmine's mind wondering if she should still go to the carnival, at least to support a local organization. She reaffirmed to herself she would attend, and hoped if a tunnel of love ride were there, whoever operated it won't use it to suck her in and attempt to trap her.

About the Author

Teresa Edmond-Sargeant is an award-winning journalist and author. Her work in New Jersey and Florida newspapers has garnered her three press association awards in both states. Her short stories have appeared in several publications including the Demonic Anthology series, "Thrill of the Hunt: Buried Alive," and 121 Words.

In speculative fiction and satire, she loves reading quirky stories with some dark humor, dialogues loaded with quips, and a central message that make her go "Hmmm ..." about life and beyond. She also loves reading inspirational/spiritual books, stories containing incredible dynamics between family and other characters, and the occasional historical non-fiction or bio.

Besides a journalist and author, she is also an art/culture/history junkie, shopping enthusiast, and church and community volunteer. She also loves her husband and their daughters, who they know will grow up to be confident and compassionate women.

Facebook, Twitter, and Instagram: @teresaesargeant

Author Amazon page: www.amazon.com/author/teresaesargeant

Website: www.teresa-edmond-sargeant.com

It isn't Bobby

Erika Lance

"I'm telling you. It's NOT my Bobby." Gina said to Taylor, twirling her bleached hair that used to be pink but was now a sort of rose tinted yellow. The girls were sitting in a booth at Gloria's Diner drinking a milkshake and eating what remained of a plate of fries.

Taylor sighed, grabbing another fry and dunking it into a glob of ketchup before putting it in her mouth. When she was mostly finished chewing, she said "Why do you think he's not YOUR Bobby?" she then shrugged, "He looks exactly the same to me."

"It's not how he looks..." Gina started sounding angry, "It's how he is acting."

"Acting?" Taylor asked grabbing another fry.

Gina looked around the diner to see if anyone she cared about - which is very few people - were there. "I think it was that damn ride. You know, from the carnival."

"You think he's been acting weird since he went on a ride at the carnival?" Taylor was trying to take a sip from the soda but instead made a suction noise as all that was left was ice. She held up the glass and shook it, trying to grab the waitress's attention. "Where the hell is she?" looking around. "Also, you know you sound crazy, right?" she said, putting the glass back down once the waitress nodded that she saw her.

"I am not CRAZY!" Gina said then realized how loud her voice was. "I know something happened. I just know it. He got on that stupid ride and

79

when he got off, he was... Well it wasn't normal Bobby is all."

The waitress came over to fill both their glasses with soda and asked, "Are you done with that?" gesturing to the plate of fries. "Do I look done?" Taylor retorted before sticking three more fries into her mouth which simply caused the waitress to roll her eyes and walk away.

"Ok fine." Taylor said after swallowing most of what was in her mouth "How is he different?"

"Well..." Gina started "You're probably going to think this is stupid-" she continued.

"I already think this is stupid" Taylor said under her breath.

Gina looked like she was on the brink of tears, "He walked me to school on Monday." She started to cry.

Taylor shook her head "You're sad because he walked you to school?"

"No. I'm sad because he walked me to school every day this week." Gina grabbed a napkin to wipe away the mascara running down her face now. "He has never, ever, ever, walked me to school before."

"Alright so why do you think this is linked to some ride at the carnival?"

"Because Madison said the same thing happened with Josh." Gina now looked like a raccoon as the napkin didn't absorb so much as smear the makeup around her eyes.

"What did Madison tell you?"

Still sniffling, "You know how Josh calls her fat all the time?"

"Yeah, that's why she throws up all the time," Taylor said with a smirk.

"Well the day after the ride he took her out to breakfast. She ordered like an egg whites or oatmeal and he asked her why she wasn't eating her favorite pancakes. She figured it was a trick and said she liked the oatmeal, even though nobody who isn't old likes oatmeal." She wiped at her eyes.

"And?"

"And he bought her pancakes."

Taylor shook her head "I'm still not seeing what is wrong. So, he fed her. That's not a grand gesture."

"I know. But... he not only fed her, he didn't call her fat, or a pig, or a heifer, or any of the other horrible things he used to call her every day. And, he brought her candy every day last week." Gina sounded almost out of breath she was talking so fast.

"Ok, so Maddy's getting free food and you're getting walked to school. These are still not earth-shattering situations. Did anything else happen? Something big? Something anyone other than you two would consider a big deal?"

"Bobby hasn't hit me once since Saturday!" Gina blurted out and started sobbing again.

"He hit you?" Taylor sounded shocked.

Gina looked down at her hands on her lap under the table, "Yeah. He used to hit me when I made him mad. Or sometimes when other people, like his parents or teachers made him mad too." She shrugged, "He didn't mean to. He would tell me he was sorry. Just... He did it on account of him having so much responsibility with being Captain of the baseball team and all."

Taylor didn't say anything at first. She bit at the inside of her lip.

"I'm sorry," Gina said, still not looking up.

"For?"

"I... I... I shouldn't have said anything."

"Why do you say that?" Taylor asked confused.

Gina shrugged her shoulders "Because Bobby wouldn't have...."

"It doesn't matter what the fuck that asshole would want," Taylor's voice rose, "He can get hit by a bus or something. God what a dick!"

Gina finally looked back up, "I know. But he's changed."

Taylor folded her arms and looked away, "You said that before."

Gina went quiet.

After a minute Taylor pointed at Gina and smiled, "You look like a raccoon".

Gina got up from the booth and headed to the bathroom. Taylor took another sip from her soda and pulled out a mirror and gloss. She checked to make sure that nothing was in her teeth, or on her face and reapplied the plum shimmer to her lips.

The waitress walked up and dropped the check on table and simply walked away, taking none of the dirty dishes with her.

"Bitch." Taylor mumbled under her breath. Looked at the check it was for $12.54. She put down $13.00 just as Gina walked up then stood up herself. "Ready?" and headed for the door.

As they both got into Taylor's Jeep, Gina asked, "Where are we going?"

"Carnival." Taylor said as she started the Jeep and put on her seatbelt. "It's here for one more day, we should see if this ride is melting people's minds."

They headed towards the edge of town where the carnival had been set-up. It was in a field near the old tractor dealership. As they arrived there were a few people around, but it looked like most of the workers were just hanging out.

"Where is everyone?" Gina asked as they got out of the Jeep.

"Maybe they've all been brainwashed to be nice and so they're out walking kids to school."

Taylor replied as she locked the doors.

"There isn't school on Saturday." Gina replied.

Taylor glared at her and proceeded to walk up to the ticket booth.

There was a boy that didn't look much older than fourteen with a mullet wearing overalls.

'Could he be more of a stereotype.' Taylor thought as she scanned the ride sign. She spotted Alien Invasion on the list. It required four tickets.

"Four tickets." She said pulling out a ten and sliding it through the little window. The boy smiled, with only about six teeth she could see and said with a southern accent, "You can get twenty tickets for ten dollars." And with that, he completed the stereotype for Taylor.

"Fine." Taylor replied and took the tickets as she slid them through the window.

They made their way down the midway. There were all the normal games, ball toss, break the balloon, the water gun game, but each one looked run down and pathetic to Taylor. The people manning them were even worse.

The whistling and catcalling started almost immediately, and Gina would smile over in their direction. Which of course caused the offenders to try to lure them over to play a game or "just come chat with me, sweetie."

It made Taylor nauseous and finally she had to grab Gina's arm "Stop it!" with eyes wide "We are here to see what happened to your stupid boyfriend and these people are disgusting."

"Sorry..." Gina said in a low voice.

Taylor let go of Gina's arm but realized when looking at her friend that this must be what she looked like when Bobby hit her.

"I'm sorry. I just don't want any of that," gesturing to the dirty man loading up beer bottles onto the rack and leering in their direction, "to come anywhere near us. Ok?"

Gina nodded and they headed towards the rides.

The Alien Invasion wasn't hard to find. It was the only ride that was shaped like a spaceship. When Taylor took a moment to look at it, she wasn't surprised about a third of the lights being out on the sign so at night it simply read "Invasion."

She walked toward where the line would form and realized Gina had stopped.

She turned around, "Come on!" but Gina shook her head.

Taylor turned around and walked back up to her. "What?"

"I don't want to go in there." Gina stared at the ride.

"Why not?"

"Look what it did to Bobby and Josh." Gina sounded a little afraid.

"You mean, make them better people?" Taylor raise her arms and wiggled her fingers "Oooo... So terrifying. You are being stupid, come on." Making her way back towards the ride. Gina hesitated for a moment then followed.

They handed the tickets to a lovely girl who was wearing ripped jeans and an Insane Clown Posse shirt with at least three unintentional holes and a few stains.

She looked at them, spit on the ground to her left, and asked "Just you two?" with a huge mound of tobacco in one cheek.

"Yep. Just us." Taylor replied cringing a little.

The girl nodded in the direction of the entrance.

Taylor walked up into the open door from the ship. Inside, it was dark with little lights running around the top of the 'ship' and down the sides to indicate where each person should stand. It was cold in comparison to the temperature outside, most likely trying to keep it comfortable for when they crammed thirty people in here. It also smelled like moldy dried sweat.

Taylor covered her mouth "Don't they ever clean this place?" She pointed to a spot across from the one she was standing at. "Go stand there. That way we can see each other."

Gina complied but still looked scared.

A voice came over the speakers that sounded like a cheesy alien you see in cartoons. "Welcome Earthlings" the lights around the top of the room began to speed up. "To ensure you are not injured please keep your back against the wall during the duration of the ride. Also, do not attempt to climb up the wall. This could cause serious injury. Enjoy your trip."

With that the entire room went dark, Gina squeaked.

Then the room began to move, slowly at first it began to spin in a circle. It was almost instinct to close her eyes. Taylor yelled "Gina keep your eyes open".

"Why? It's dark" and as if answering her question there were lights that began to light up near the top of the ship.

They were dull at first, almost pulsing, then slowly they became brighter and as Taylor looked up, she noticed the lights were coming from a spiderweb of strands that were in various sizes and lengths. They seemed almost messy but if the lights were not pulsing through them you wouldn't have seen them along the black ceiling.

The ride began to move faster and that is when Taylor first saw the movement on one of the strands. At first, she thought it was because the room was spinning and the light was playing tricks but its second arm emerged, pulling itself along one of the strands. It had what looked like three fingers, the middle one being a claw.

Taking a deep breath, with effort she looked over at Gina. Her eyes were closed. "GINA!" she tried to scream but there was no sound, just the music from the ride.

When she looked up again the creature was farther along. It had a head like a mantis, and now she could see four arms. Because of the moving lights she couldn't tell how far away from her the creature was to determine how large it was. Moving in and out of the strands she also couldn't see its body, but it was moving towards Gina.

The ride picked up speed. Taylor was now pushed against the wall. Her head held in place just looking at this thing moving toward her friend. She tried to open her mouth to scream again to the same result. The creature was now perched above Gina's head. Its spade shaped body was clear with lines of black running through it. It had a long thin spike for a tail, which it moved to be directly above Gina's head.

It struck downward, plunging the spike into the top of Gina's skull. Her eyes opened and were looking directly at Taylor.

Taylor tried again to pull herself from the wall as the creature turned its head to look at her. It pushed itself deeper into Gina's head. Two of its claws hooking under Gina's chin.

Taylor wanted to turn her gaze from her friend. 'What have I done? Gina hadn't wanted to be here.'

The creature's belly began to pulse as liquids began to move around. It moved its other two arms to hold it in place as the pulling got faster. Gina's eyes began to flutter until they closed.

Tears began to run down Taylor's face. Her friend slumped and the creature began to pull itself out of the top of Gina's head. When the spike was fully removed, the creature put its head closer to the hole and something round dropped from the creature's mouth into the hole.

Taylor felt herself wanting to throw up.

The lights went out and the ride began to slow. When it stopped, the door opened, and the room returned to its original lighting. The creature gone.

She raced over towards Gina, "Oh my God, Oh my God, Oh my...." she was cut off when Gina looked up at her, "What's wrong?" she said.

"Wait." Taylor grabbed Gina's head to look at the top.

"Ouch!" Gina exclaimed "What's wrong with you?" she said trying to pull out of Taylor's grasp.

Taylor held on and looked at her head. There was nothing there. No hole. No mark. No scar. She let go. Turning around, she looked up again. In the corner she saw a small pulse of light and it went black again. They hurried towards the door and as they emerged into the light, they passed the ticket taker for the ride who only nodded and spit again. Taylor was breathing hard and she looked behind her as they walked hurriedly away from the ride. She turned to look at Gina, who looked the same as she did when they arrived.

"Are you ok?" Gina asked.

"I'm fine. Just a little...." Taylor wasn't sure what to say. She wanted to say, 'Afraid something put an alien inside your head.' Her heart was racing.

"Yeah, I hate those rides." Gina continued as they moved towards the car, "they always give me a headache. At least there weren't any aliens, huh?"

Taylor turned and threw up.

ABOUT THE AUTHOR

Erika had the unique opportunity to live in several different environments across the country growing up, giving her a colorful perspective on life. Born in Minnesota, she spent most of her formative years in Hollywood, then a ranch in New Mexico on the border of an Indian reservation. With a love of the arts since she was a child (acting, painting, sewing and dancing to name a few!) she found her passion in writing. Beginning with short stories, poems and articles for local papers. Remember, not every story has a happy ending.

www.erikalance.com

Twitter: AuthorELance

FaceBook: www.facebook.com/pages/authorelance

Instagram: AuthorELance

Cervantees the Puppet Master

F.D. Gross

Jack Dresden tore into his turkey leg with grim satisfaction. Juices dripped down his stubbly chin as he looked around the fairgrounds, searching for the next stand that would yield him another Black and Tan.

Ah yes, the South Florida Fair. He came here every year. It was like a tradition for him, meeting with his group of friends all dressed in black in the parking lot and entering the grounds together like that one scene from Tombstone. But this year was different. This was his third year away at college, and ever since high school, the group began to die off, getting smaller and smaller as time went on, each of them getting sucked into the work force or moving away to some other college. Now completely alone this summer, Jack decided to make the best of it, by drinking as much beer possible and trying his luck with the local girls. Possibly pull off a summer fling.

Jack's head spun looking at all the rides and carnival games as he walked the aisles, smelling the sweet scents of popping corn and French fries. Taking a deep breath, the humidity mixed with the fair ground's exhaust made him cough. He choked it back as best he could while tearing up, and it was immediately after this that he noticed the sound that would change his life forever. The voice of a lovely female, singing to her heart's content. The soprano vocals wafted through the air like the sweet smell of elephant ears.

He followed that sound, gently pushing past a group of teenage girls giggling while covering their mouths and past an elderly couple holding hands, sharing a paper bag of cinnamon twists. He didn't notice any of them. Not one bit.

What he did notice was the strange looking black tent with red stripes. It loomed before him like a menacing demon mouth ready to devour. Dark and foreboding, he knew it was very different from the rest of the fair. He'd never seen it before.

He paused at the threshold of a ten-foot flap drawn closed. Just above it, a large sign in bold English letters read "Cervantees the Puppet Master presents: The Saga of Assassin Maleena." *Puppet master? A puppeteer here at the fair?* This was certainly a first, thought Jack. Strangely enough, he always had a fascination for puppets and ventriloquism. He grew up on Jim Henson films like the *Labyrinth* and the *Dark Crystal*, and now his curiosity was peaked. Conscious his mouth was open, he quickly closed it while reading another sign just to the right of it which read: "Caution: You may get wet."

"Yeah, that's normal," said Jack sarcastically, taking another bite of his turkey leg and spitting out a tendon. "Well, I definitely gotta see this," and just as he was about to enter the tent, a sharp pain exploded in his shoulder. He came to his senses. "Ow! Jesus!"

"That's not my name," said a quivering voice. "It's Henry, and you have to pay, bub."

Jack turned his head and didn't see anyone until he lowered his gaze and saw an old hunchback man hobbling back and forth on his feet, tapping his stick on the ground like a showman. The codgy old fella called Henry smirked at Jack through his massively framed, thick magnified bifocals; the background glare from the carnival's colored lights distorted any chance at revealing his eyes. "You deaf, bub? You gotta pay," said Henry again as if Jack didn't hear him.

"Pay?" Jack was still trying to process why this little old man struck him.

"Can't you read the sign? It's ten bucks to enter." Henry pointed at an empty part of the canvas wall instead of the ten-dollar sign.

What the hell. They have an old blind guy manning the ticket booth. Jesus.

Quickly, he handed Henry a ten-dollar bill and went into the tent to avoid being hit again.

Stepping into the tent was like vanishing into a spectral portal. The aisles, dimly lit with those fake flickering candles they sell at arts and craft stores, were hard enough to see let alone the many chairs his shins suffered from with every step he took. They were all empty from what he could tell except for the audience up front, as close as they could get to the stage. A female figure, a puppet almost the size of an actual human, stood in the middle of the stage, singing in a soft tone, bathed in blue and red stage lights. There was no mistake the voice Jack heard was hers, or rather, the puppeteer conveniently hidden behind the curtains. So beautiful the sound was it stirred something within Jack which made him uncomfortable at first, but then relaxed. The female puppet, all dressed in white with a white hood held a bouquet of red roses before her while twirling around the stage. As weird as it was, Jack instantly connected with the puppet. A strange feeling passed through his body. The curvy detail of her outfit. The supple blonde locks sprouting from underneath her hood. *Man,* he thought to himself. *She looks so real!*

Jack took a seat at the back and noticed how all of the spectators were wearing white t-shirts over their regular outfits as if they were part of some strange ritual.

The female puppet stopped singing and the lights went out, engulfing the stage in pitch blackness. A few moments passed and the lights came back on. Now everything could be seen in detail and the scene changed drastically. The female puppet in white had her hands bound behind her back and was surrounded by other puppets dressed in medieval armor. At the far left of the stage, a fat puppet dressed like a king sat on a throne. He held a scroll of parchment before him while the puppeteer behind the stage threw his voice to make it sound as if the king were speaking. *This Cervantees certainly has talent.*

"I do here decree, the white widow of Yorkenhime be slayed where she stands for crimes committed in collusion with the devil. Acts of murder will not go unpunished in our holy kingdom. By fortitude will I uphold these laws. So help us God." The king lowered his parchment. "Does the *Assassin* Maleena have any final words before the sentence is carried out?" The king's words hung in the air like poison.

Maleena bowed her head and called out for all to hear. "Is there nothing I can say that will change your minds?" She turned to the audience, her words pleading. "Has hope died within all of you?"

Silence hung in the stale air. Jack listened to the audience members breathing. Someone was sucking their soda through a straw. Then, one of the guardsmen drew his sword and moved behind Assassin Maleena.

Jack sensed the tension in the crowd.

Without warning, the guardsmen thrust his lifelike blade. But the sword never struck Maleena, for in that instant, her hands became unbound and while sidestepping, caught the blade between her hands, and forced the guard's momentum forward. The tip of the sword buried deep in the torso of another sentry, sending copious amounts of blood spraying across an elated audience. Mass applause broke from the crowd as they stood up from their seats. Voices erupted from the stage all at once, yelling and screaming, Maleena shouting the words "justice" and "freedom," and the king yelling profanity and the phrase "Kill her! Kill her!"

There must be more than one puppeteer back there! Has to be!

The audience continued to be bathed in blood and gore, as Maleena slashed the throat of a guard and rammed a hidden knife in the back of another. More blood speckled smiling faces.

Jesus Christ. What kind of show was this? Jack tasted cherry on his lips, some of it landed on his shirt.

Suddenly the lights dimmed, fading to a solo red and the audience settled back down into their seats. A violin played over the speakers, filling the inside of tent with a hallowed tune. Jack watched, with anticipation or horror, he wasn't quite sure, as Maleena approached the king face to face.

"What is this!" shouted the king. "Who are you!" The invisible strings obviously making the king quiver in his stance as Maleena ascended the steps one by one.

She stopped just before him and simply said, "I am the assassin Maleena, and I am death, come to change the world, one dead king at a time." She slashed his throat and a line of blood spurted from the open cavity of his neck, spraying those in the front row. The act of it looked so real yet they were just puppets. Weren't they?

The crowd burst into standing ovation as the curtain drew to a close.

What the hell did I just watch?

Moments later, the curtain opened again to reveal what Jack thought would be an entourage cast of puppeteers, but such was not the case. Standing alone on the stage stood a figure, the one responsible for the absurd, brilliant show. Cervantees. Tall and lanky and head covered in cowl and mask, a black trench coat hung from his broad shoulders, surely built to uphold the pulling and stretching of strings to lift those heavy puppets. Then, deeply bowing to the audience, the curtain closed once more and the lights came on.

CERVANTEES THE PUPPET MASTER BY F.D. GROSS

As the crowd dispersed, some of them moved to a wall covered in puppets for sale. Jack noticed the reason why the crowd had worn the white shirts in the first place. The blood sprayed from the show stained their shirts, some thicker than others. He listened as they commented on the patterns as if they were works of art. This night would never be forgotten some of them said. It was only now he realized the old man from the ticket booth, Henry, manned the merchant booth, exchanging the puppet dolls with knives in their hands, for money.

Bewildered, Jack couldn't stop thinking about Maleena, how beautifully crafted she was. Her golden hair. Her fair skin. Her bloodstained outfit. He had to see her up close, see her construction, touch her and run his fingers through those golden locks of humanlike hair. Also, he wanted to congratulate this Cervantees personally, let him know just how brilliant he was. Yet the inside of the tent grew quiet after sales were made, and the curtain remained shut. He made his way up to the stage, trying to peer between the black curtains. Not seeing anything, he moved closer to the edge, trying to catch sight of Cervantees and what secrets he hid. And just when he thought his time had run out, before the old man returned with the stick, he found a way into the backstage—after moving some French barricades.

Jack envisioned, just beyond the flap of curtains, he would see it all. He was sure of it. As his hands moved the curtain, the gaunt face of Cervantees appeared in the darkness. Dressed in black attire, his head seemed to float without a body. "What do you want?"

Cervantee's voice sounded like that of a hissing reptile. *Impossible!* Thought Jack. *How could his voice sound so harsh when earlier his voice sounded like an opera singer?*

"You're not supposed to be back here," spat Cervantees. "Get out!"

Jack didn't know what to say. So taken by his rudeness, he staggered back a few paces, bumping into the barricade with a loud rattle. "Hey, sorry man. I was just looking to meet you and tell you how awesome of a show that was—"

Cervantees glared at Jack as if he were a meal for a lion. "Trying to steal my secrets?" he asked in his harsh rasp. "Trying to get a good peek at the assassin Maleena, are you? If you don't get out of here right now, bad things might happen. I'll call Henry in with the stick—"

Jack didn't know why he said it, but he said it anyway, blurting out the one thing that sounded absurd, yet knew the feeling was real. "Teach me.

I want to learn what you know. I want to be your apprentice!"

Cervantees stopped dead in his belittling and sized up Jack with his puffy eyes. Jack could tell the gears were turning, but whether it was for the better or worse, he wasn't sure.

"Ha!" belted Cervantes, his head disappeared in the darkness. "I don't take on apprentices!"

The next day, Jack returned in the evening, determined to land a job with Cervantees the Puppet Master. He didn't care what he had to do as long as it got his foot in the door and got him closer to seeing the lifelike dolls that stayed behind the black curtain. Especially Maleena. He paid his ten dollars while being glared at by Henry and entered into the tent to watch the same show he witnessed the night before. This time, he got to see the whole performance, while conveniently sitting up front with his white shirt and all. It was a strange feeling being sprayed with blood periodically throughout the performance, tasting the familiar cherry on his lips. He watched like a hawk, wiping the blood from his face and watching the changes in the scenes, the impossible efficiency of it, how quickly it was done and flawlessly.

At the end of the performance, again, the same motions occurred. Ecstatic customers with overzealous enthusiasm of purchasing more dolls. With Henry overwhelmed and distracted by the overbearing crowd, Jack again decided to somehow confront Cervantees and ask for an apprenticeship. He saw his chance when a black cloaked figure emerged from behind the stage and bolted straight out the front of the tent. *It has to be him!*

Quickly Jack followed, pushing past distracted buyers, and emerging into the night of sweet cotton candy and flashing lights. The standard clown-at-the-circus-music was playing somewhere in the distance. The corner of his eye caught a glimpse of a fluttering black cloak passing around the backside of the tent and into an alleyway of extension cords and old boxes spewing Styrofoam. So Jack followed.

Utterly dark and desolate behind the tent, Jack didn't care for his safety. He watched the cloaked figure make its way to an unlit trailer with its blinds drawn shut.

"Cervantees! Wait!"

The cloaked figure turned on the spot and flashed a 9mm Glock at Jack.

Cervantees the Puppet Master by F.D. Gross

"Whoa, Jesus, man! Easy pal, it's me, the guy from last night. Jack... Jack Dresden."

The cloaked figure's hood gazed upward. "Do you always go following after people into dark alleyways, Jack Dresden?" The unmistakable raspy voice of Cervantees seethed at the tongue.

"No, I don't. But I'm desperate. I mean—what I'm trying to say is, ever since last night..." Jack paused running his hand through his hair. "I don't know man. The voices you use, the realness of the puppets...it's just so... *incredible*. Really, no joke. It's like I feel compelled to work for you. I want to become a puppeteer just like you."

A scoffing sound came from Cervantees as he stowed the gun in his clothes and pulled back the hood. "A puppeteer like me. Do you have any idea, Jack Dresden, what it's like to be a puppeteer? A *real* puppeteer?" His beady eyes flashed in what little light there was in that dark alley. "Dedication. Sacrifice. Copious amounts of...sacrifice." His gaze dropped to the floor.

"Not a problem. I can do that." The eagerness in Jack's eyes was apparent and he felt that he convinced Cervantees somehow.

After a momentary pause, Cervantees drew a breath and said, "Fine. You can start tomorrow. Mr. Henry will give you the details." And with that, Cervantees staggered up the stairs of his trailer and slammed the door.

Jack did it. He actually pulled it off.

Already a week had gone by and Jack was in the swing of things, apprenticed by the Great Cervantees, the Puppet Master, or so he thought in his mind anyway. After meeting with Henry a week ago, he started with selling tickets at the ticket counter outside the tent, the very spot where Henry assaulted him with the stick. He rarely saw Cervantees in his comings and goings, but that didn't matter. After a week had gone by, Henry had him ushering the crowd in, showing them their seats, and assisting with the selling of white shirts behind the inside counter. Henry explained that not long ago, the girl who was selling the shirts just up and left one day, no warning, no explanation.

Jack tried not to worry about the time that was slowly ebbing away from him. Already with the fair having been in town for two weeks, it meant there were only two weeks left before they uprooted and moved on to Tampa, Florida. Would Cervantees the Puppet Master be going as well? As he sat behind the counter, justifying his decision to stay—that he still had a month or so before he'd have to go back to school—a familiar sharp pain brought him back to the now.

"Jack! A customer!" retorted Henry with the stick in his hand.

"S-sorry," said Jack as he handed out another white shirt to an overly eager paying customer. *How long* he thought to himself. *How long do they keep me selling shirts and dolls?* But an answer never came for him.

It wasn't until the end of the third week that Jack Dresden's wishes were finally culled. One night, after the performance was done, and Cervantees finished his brief bowing, and the crowd had dispersed out the tent back into the fray of carnival screams and frying oil, Jack heard his name being called during his nightly sweeping. It was Henry who was calling his name in the strangest of ways, almost as a whisper, barely audible to the naked ear. It made Jack's skin crawl, but he responded obediently and made his way behind the French barricades to the side of the stage where Henry's head poked between the black curtains. *This is it!* Jack thought, setting down his broom and waiting patiently.

"Master Cervantees wanted me to tell you, you have proven your worth. Your hours of hard work and dedication have shown him you are worth his time. Please enter."

Passing beyond the threshold of the black curtains was bliss for Jack. So long he waited for the chance to see Cervantees' craft and hidden secrets, he was beside himself. Full of the good kind of anxiety, he didn't know what to expect as Henry smiled, nodded, and left him to his faculties.

It was nothing like how he imagined it. Nylon strings and pulleys hung from various corners of the tent as Jack entered the low-lit theater that was Cervantee's domain. All the puppets he'd seen from the performances were there, lined up in a fashionable way with their arms to their sides, and their bodies stripped down to the plush pleather they were made of. Maleena, the star of the show, sat before a vanity mirror with her back toward Jack as if prepping herself for the next performance. Again, how real she looked to him as he made his way into the center of the room. On a shelf lingering not too far away sat a trunk made of ivory white, bejeweled with brilliant blue sapphires sparkling in the candle light.

"It's called the roamer's chest," came Cervantees voice from across the room. "It was a gift from a circus ringleader in India long ago. It's said to bring good fortune." Cervantees emerged from the shadows like billowing smoke. "It holds all of my biggest secrets. A real chest of treasure."

Jack swallowed hard but stood his ground. He didn't want to show Cervantees a break in his confidence.

"I realized that next week is the final week the fair will be in town and here we are, and I never showed you any of the things that I do. So," he said, crossing his arms and leaning against the trunk, "Are you ready?"

The week went by as a blur and Jack's apprenticeship was almost over. Cervantees showed him so much. The invisible nylon strings that never refracted in the angled lights. The army of puppets, with their swords and armor, the fat king and his throne. Maleena, the star of the show, her golden hair and smooth doll skin. He got to touch them all, buff them to a shine and comb their knotted hair. There was the fake cherry blood used to fill the puppets on their backside, the breakaway tears where the blades tore open the stitches. The mending and the cleaning of body parts and the shining of their beady glass eyes. They ate and drank and worked their arms out on the pulleys and nylon strings. Jack was getting the royal treatment, everything that came with being a puppeteer all the while in the presence of the great Cervantees. And not once did he question the "things" building up inside his head, especially about Cervantee's biggest and best-kept secret—throwing his voice as if he were multiple people at once. Never was Jack allowed behind the curtains during performances but was granted immediate access thereafter. Henry would just laugh in the background as Jack dragged the dolls backstage.

On the last night, after the final performance was over and all the people had left, Cervantees came up to Jack to thank him one last time. Sweat dripped from his brow.

"It saddens me that we will be leaving tomorrow. Never have I seen such determination and eagerness in a pupil such as you, Jack Dresden. You are truly a marvel."

"I thought you didn't take on apprentices," said Jack with a wry smile. Cervantees stared at Jack as if waiting for something. There seemed to be a blue glow coming from his eyes.

DEMONIC CARNIVAL

"Is there something you want to say, Jack Dresden?"

"Take me with you," said Jack, suddenly. It was as if a weight had been lifted from his chest.

But the relief was short-lived, and reality came back at him hard like a knife in his chest.

"Not a chance," said Cervantees. His eyes gleamed in the red and blue stage lights.

"Why not?" Jack fired back. His hurt pride recovered quickly with anger.

"Because, Jack, becoming a puppet master takes time *and* dedication. You have neither. You have your school, Jack. Don't throw your life away."

Although no one could see it in the dim light, Jack's face turned red. "You don't know me. I have both. I have determination. You said so yourself!" His voice got louder. "College doesn't start back up for a month—at the end of summer. Let me show you! I can prove myself, you'll see!"

Cervantees leaned against one of the tent poles, folding his arms. His eyes moved back and forth as if searching for something. And when he spun around, turning his back on Jack, he called over his shoulder. "Very well. Come back tomorrow morning before we leave. I will give you your final test."

The next day couldn't come quick enough. With enough clothes for two weeks packed at his side, he was sure whatever test Cervantees had planned for him he would pass. He thought about his parents, what they would say if they knew what he was doing, but quickly shrugged it off. Who cares what they'd say? He was a grown adult in college, and he would be gone for a month, making it back just in time to start up classes again.

Jack smirked to himself as he looked up at the sign outside the tent 'You may get wet'. *What's wrong with doing what I want to do? It's times like this you have to live a little. Get a little* wet. *And I'm doing just that.*

It was strange entering the tent and not being greeted by Henry. As Jack looked around, a majority of the chairs, tables, dolls and stage lights had been packed away. The back curtains, separating the stage from the front, however, were still up. He made his way there, passing through the flaps that granted him access to Cervantees' private world of dolls and incense.

The small haven greeted him like always; Cervantees at the far end of the room with his back facing Jack. The dolls were lined up, all facing the center of the room as if waiting to watch a performance. His performance.

"I'm here," said Jack timidly, still holding the duffle bag at his side.

"The test has already begun," replied Cervantees.

Jack wasn't sure what to make of it and plopped his bag on the ground. "What do I have to do?"

"It's a simple task, really," said Cervantees. He never turned around to face Jack. "Open the chest and tell me what you see..."

Cervantees words trailed off as Jack's attention focused on the ivory chest faceted with the blue sapphires. *Easy enough* he thought. He had been wondering what was inside the chest this whole time. Maybe some written journals of Cervantees' past plays, or perhaps, another puppet he's been waiting to show him.

Jack placed his hands on the lid. It was cold to the touch despite the south Florida heat. Giving it a tug, the trunk opened with resistance. *What is that?* Blue light seeped from the cracked lid as it swirled about in the darkness.

A voice seemed to whisper from the everywhere. "What do you see, Jack? Tell me..."

Already committed, Jack pushed the trunk open. He could barely speak as his eyes widen. "I see...I see...me."

All at once, multiple voices came at Jack. They called his name. Cursed his name. Congratulated him while whispering in his ears. As the blue light faded, Jack stared down at his hands that were somewhat different—they were stiff like pleather.

"Has hope died within you?" said a voice to his left. It was soft and beautiful and when Jack looked up from realizing his skin wasn't real anymore, he saw the Assassin Maleena *moving* towards him, real as ever. She was alive as well as the rest of the puppet cast. The guards. The king. They were all staring at him as he tried to speak from the hollow of his chest. But no words ever came.

"Your voice will come in time," said Cervantees from the back. Jack could see Cervantee's glowing blue eyes in the dark as he approached. He began to clap and the rest followed suit.

"You passed the test," laughed Cervantees the puppet master. "Welcome to the troupe."

ABOUT THE AUTHOR

F. D. Gross is the creator and writer of The Wolfgang Trilogy series, Wolfgang and Inquisition, and is currently working on his third book. A new legend in vampire hunting begins.

Frank is a writer of many things and resides in South Florida with his wife, daughter, and three cats. You can find out more about his mysteries and horrors at www.wolfgangchronicles.com. Follow Frank's author profile on Amazon.com and check out the many reviews of his work on Goodreads.com.

Don't Make Waves

Charlotte Platt

"It's too goddamn warm," Frankie said, puffing air up his face and knocking damp curls away for a beat. They returned, limp, to plaster against his forehead.

"It's August, d'you want snow?" Sally snorted, biting into her candy floss. The woman spinning it had been an eyeful, all tattoos and acid green hair, and she kept stealing glances back at the sugar siren.

"No, I want to go on a water ride so I can cool down, dingus."

"That's a fair point," Sally said, stuffing the last of her spun snack in her mouth. "What about that one?" She pointed to the remains of a decrepit castle in a dark lake at the far end of the carnival, the water almost purple with the overcast day. There was a patchy line beside the railings and the thunder crack of water rippled over the screams and noise of the other rides.

"I've not been on log flumes in ages, that'd be great," Frankie said, nodding.

They plodded through the crowd, past giggling children and the hissing fat of the food frying stalls. Sally hummed her approval at the smell of candy apples and waffles, being dragged away by Frankie when she lingered too long at the donut selection.

"Spoil sport."

"You can eat your heart out after the ride, no eating before swimming."

"You're not meant to dive into the water, Frankie," Sally said, raising a brow at him.

"Best to be prepared," he replied with a shrug.

They looked up at the edifice of the crumbling building soaking in the moat, tufts of shredded greenery poking out from cracks. A car splashed into the far side of the water, screams accompanying the crash, and they turned to wander into the gate house styled booth.

A skinny rail of a man peered at them from the admission booth, dressed in a dark green tunic and with a smear of fake blood going from lip to chin. Arcs of rust brown were smattered over his chest and his dirty blonde hair was mussed as if he had been in a brawl, while a fake sword sat precariously on the edge of the counter.

"Welcome to the tour of the battlefield," he said, a purring lilt of an accent sparking Frankie's eyes up. "This ride is not recommended for those under the influence of any substances, or too young to appreciate the tempers of war."

"Well if there's one thing my sister can do it's fight her way to the food, I've seen things you wouldn't believe at the Christmas table," Frankie said, leaning an elbow on the counter so he could show off his muscles.

"I've got to, otherwise you'd eat it all and then cry about it," Sally said, swinging one hip into his to knock him off his ridiculous pose.

"It sounds like you're well-seasoned, then," the ticket keeper said, smirking at the pair. His eyes were coffee dark in the gloom of the little space, flicking over them in curiosity. "You can have a boat to yourselves, if you wish, or wait for others to join you."

"It's so dreadfully hot, I say we just go for our own," Frankie said, batting his lashes at Sally. She rolled her eyes but nodded.

"Wonderful. You're not permitted to put your hands outside of the boat, so no splashing, but I do recommend keeping an ear out for the waterfall: it's a breath-taking drop."

He stepped out from behind the booth, leading them through a decaying arch towards glass diffused light and the slap of water. A small boat sat, tapping against its mooring in a disrupted stable with holes in the walls for the water way, and he offered them both a hand to get in. Frankie went first, locking fingers with their guide and grinning to Sally when she hopped in behind him.

"Can you come along with us?" Frankie asked as the guide put a foot against the side of their craft. "What if we get spooked?"

"Alas, I've already been through the battle," he said, running a hand down his chest to show the fake blood. "Do come and let me know if you see anything worth a second tour, though."

With that he shoved them off and they caught on the current of the dark water, clipping into the wooden sides here and there. They emerged from the stable into an ambling river, dappled with the low sunlight breaking through clouds. A short distance ahead the false castle approached, screams erupting inside.

"Do you think it'll all be inside, like at Disney?" Frankie called, leaning back to be heard.

"Maybe? He mentioned a waterfall, they're usually external!" Sally called back against the rush of air and bite of spray now starting to clip the sides of the boat. It bobbed and dipped in the current, speeding up at the corners that swung them to and fro in the boat, curls of white foam slipping under them as they bounced in their seats.

The castle was all dark stone and ominous music, the straining strings of some knock off classical rendition interspaced with creaking wood and the clashes of metal. They were tipped down a short drop, the water splashing up and soaking them both with a sudden bite. A wave darted ahead of them, curling round the path and disappearing into the gloom.

"Welcome to the remains of the battle," a disembodied voice boomed, backed by groaning. "Their pitiful defences fell before our hordes as snow does before the righteous sun, and now we loot and finish our duty."

They were submerged into the darkness inside the castle as a hiss of pressurised air shot down from above, cold as frost and making Sally shriek. Frankie cackled at her and swung one hand back to pat her knee.

"I'll scare off anything that comes to get you, promise."

"Yeah they'd take one look at your face and bolt," she said, rubbing her arms with her hands to lift the chill. They could see a red tinged light up ahead, the peeking opening of a tunnel maybe, and the crash of weapons sounded behind them as they bumped along. Something splashed into the water beside the boat, drenching them, and then began to moan.

"The survivors are being hunted, they shall not escape their judgement," the voice above intoned as they were pulled into the fiery area, "They will join their dead in the pit."

The space was stuffed full of dioramas, bleeding light and sound and screams out over them as they bobbed past: massacres, soldiers fighting, fires raging in rooms with people trapped, giant cauldrons boiling out to spill their slick contents over boat as it rushed away. A smell of rot and burning, like someone had thrown green wood on a fire, rolled over them as they whisked past the image of a king being quartered, head popping at jaunty angle that sent the crown tumbling with a metallic clink.

"What the shit is this?" Frankie yelped, flinging himself away hard and bouncing them off the side only to shudder towards the grotesques again. They were dragged through a chain and cobweb fence, the dull slap of things dropping behind them joining with the agonised groans drifting over.

"Our battle has been a long one," the voice continued, and they began to climb a steep hill, a slick rivulets of red trickling down at them. Flashes began to pop either side of them, green and white glimpses of bodies hanging: lynchings and gallows and cages with bones and more grasping out at them. Sally screamed as one of the eyeless faces turned to follow them, pops of light tracking its movement as it struggled to raise a mangled arm. "We will show no mercy and no quarter to those not worthy of our glory."

They bumped through a wooden gate and levelled into a plateau, the water thicker and studded with lumps that knocked the boat but gave way as they rushed forward. Candlelight flickered into burning torches, showing red water running underneath and the lumps became bodies, floating face down with arrows and worse studded through their backs. The music had fallen away, just the sound of the current and Sally's shaking breath bouncing back at them. A metallic smell blossomed, thick and cloying, as the way ahead began to choke with the scrum of limbs.

"Frankie, what the fuck?" Sally whispered, clinging to his shoulders as they slowed a little, the crunch of bones striking against them as their vessel ploughed on through. A struggling gurgle sounded ahead and one of the bodies wrenched itself up, a shuddering gasp ripping through the air.

"Please, help," the figure screamed, voice hoarse, staggering towards the boat with the stunted gait of injury. "They're coming for us, they're hunting us like animals, please!" They tripped, chest thumping against the boat with a hollow thud and one hand landing on Frankie's arm with a frozen, deathly grip. The face, bloody and torn from fighting, peered at him, fetid breath spilling out. "You have to help me, this must end."

Frankie opened his mouth to shout but was cut short when a sword swung down, slicing through the head in front of him. Sally choked off a scream as Frankie jolted back in his seat, pushing himself as far away from the black blood flowing out of the body as he could. A foot landed on the shoulder, pushing it off into the water as the sword was pulled from the skull with a wet pop, and their guide peered over at them. Crouched low in the space and straddling Sally's seat, those dark eyes glowed sapphire as he intoned with a wicked grin, "No mercy, no quarter."

The sound of roaring water drowned out the whimper Frankie made as they thrust under a waterfall, crimson and hot as blood, before they were shooting down a vicious slope and into the daylight again. They skidded into the dark pool, water flying up around them, before the boat ambled along to the dock.

Sally's hands were like ice on Frankie's shoulders, grinding his muscles to mince as he scrabbled for his seatbelt and wrenched at the fastener.

"Oh god, oh fuck," he babbled, shaking with cold and shock.

"May I?" a smooth voice asked, the guide now stood on the dock and dry as a bone. There was a fresh smattering of faded blood along his side, like a sword had been wiped clean, but the blade was nowhere to be seen. He slipped his hand into the boat, unclipping the belt in one smooth movement before turning to Sally and doing the same.

"How are you here?" Sally asked, looking to the back of the craft and back again.

"There's a secret door that lets me get between the stables and the gate, it's so much easier than having two people man the ride," he said, drawling the words with a lazy grin.

"You were on the ride though," Frankie said, darting out of the boat and grabbing Sally's hand in his to pull her after him.

"No, I told you I couldn't go in again," he said with a laugh, shaking his head at them. "Though if that's your way of saying I look like one of those I should probably be offended." Sally shook her head, tightening her grip on Frankie's hand and tugging at him.

"We should go," she said, half to him and half to the guide.

"Yes, plenty more rides to enjoy. I do recommend you go and get something to eat though, it can get awful chilly when you're soaked through. Maybe something sweet, like some donuts? They always go down a treat."

"Sounds good," she said, nodding, and began to pull Frankie off to the gate.

"Oh, if I may?" the man called after them.

"Hm?" Frankie said, stopping to turn.

"Do feel free to come back for an uninterrupted ride. It's more fun when it's not interactive, I promise."

About the Author

Charlotte Platt is a young professional who writes horror and urban fantasy. She spent her teens on the Orkney Islands and studied for her profession in Glasgow, before moving up to the north Highlands for her current job. She has taken inspiration from a wide variety of sources including haunted military buildings, sceptical horses and the creeping woods that line the Thurso river. She lives off sarcasm and tea and can often be spotted walking near cliffs and rivers, looking for sea glass. She has recently had works published in Switchblade: Stiletto Heeled, Trembling With Fear and Silk+Smoke. She can be found on Twitter as @Chazzaroo or online at https://curiousfictions.com/authors/484-charlotte-platt

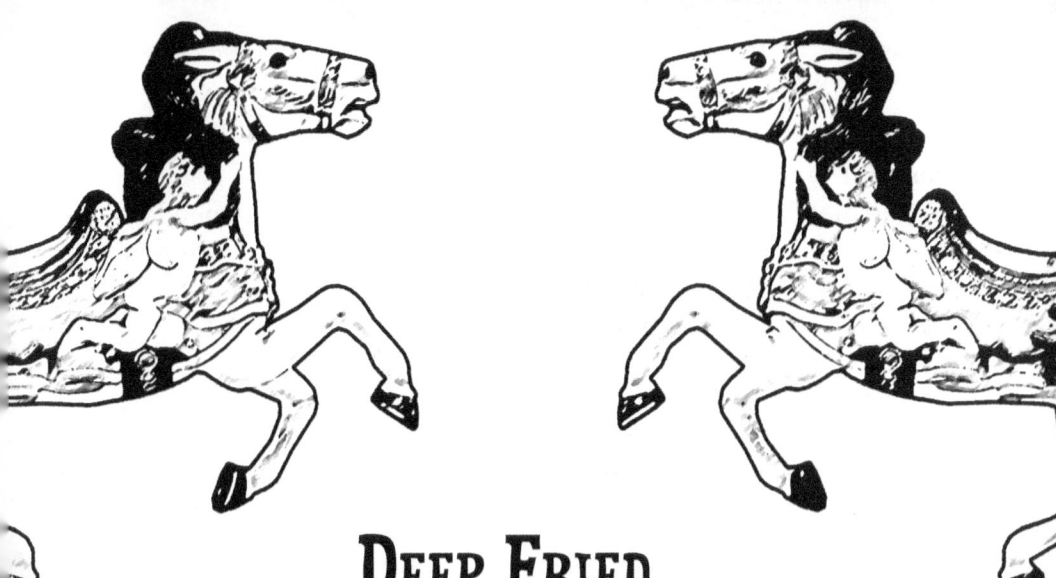

Deep Fried

George Alan Bradley

"One of 'em elephant ears..."

The man at the counter was a great breathless mountain of skin and bones, peaked with a swollen face that reminded Luby of a side of ham that had been left out for several days. His stubble-shadowed cheeks were a sour burnt red, his hair a thin buzz of reddish gray. His eyes, the color of old dishwater, probed beneath a blister of shimmering sweat, trying vainly to read the laminated menu affixed above the warm glow of the heating trays as a silky strand of saliva came rolling off the great slug of his upper lip.

"Uh, what else did I get again?"

She glanced down at the tiny faded letters on the paper. "One double-chocolate deep fried corn dog with crushed Oreo and whipped cream, large Diet Pepsi..." She paused, clicking the crusted old buttons of the register to record the dollar-fifty for the elephant ear. The keys were crusty, callused with grime like old scabs. Never cleaned, the white of the register's plastic case stained a deep mustard yellow like everything in FRIED OPEN PLAIN. "Then one bag of kettle corn with extra butter, the elephant ear, and--"

"Burger?"

"Yes sir." She handed him the ear, which Camberline had just silently laid down on the warmer. The fresh dough, doused in butter, glistened in the sun. "One cotton burger with cheese and bacon. Anything else you want?"

The man shook his head and took out his wallet. He opened it then stopped suddenly. Beside him a woman had appeared, muttering in his ear, in the mysterious way old women often muttered at older men. A worried frown crept across his face. "How much?" he asked.

"Total's fifteen-fifty."

He nodded, unsmiling, and began pulling out a twenty.

"Hold on a second!" The woman's voice was an agitated squawk, her wrinkled mouth stretched in ready outrage. "Fifteen dollars? Is that what you said?"

"Yes ma'am."

The woman looked at the man, incensed, "What the hell do you think you're doing, Wode?"

Luby winced. Already she knew what was about to happen. Had known, in fact, since the moment she had noticed that muttering.

"Well?" Her voice was loud, shrill and piercing, several passers-by stared. "Answer me, fat ass, you're about to spend fifteen bucks on some nasty food?"

"I'm hungry," the man – Wode, apparently – mewled, "what does it matter?"

"It's killing you, that's what it matters." The woman reached out and prodded his belly with a cracked pink nail. Hard sharp in the center of overflowing flesh behind the stretched cotton of his KS Wildcats t-shirt. "That's killing you, see? Idiot."

"Hey, that hurt!"

"Did it now? Surprised you can feel anything through that tank of lard." The woman giggled contemptuously and turned back to the counter, her smile vanishing into a look of accusation. "My husband, he has a condition," she said, slowly, enunciating every word, the way Luby had come to learn a lot of folks did when they saw a woman with dark skin and raven black hair in a service position, as though she hadn't just been speaking perfect English seconds before. "What can you can do?"

"I'm sorry?"

"The price!" The woman looked impatient. "Fifteen bucks...it's a lot don't you think? Especially when you know you shouldn't really be selling it - A bartender wouldn't sell liquor to a drunk, would they?"

"I--"

"I'll pay five, how's that? Seeing's as you already started makin' it."

Luby stared, wondering if the woman was joking. She wasn't. "It...it doesn't work that way."

"You're really gonna charge us fifteen bucks? Are you friggin' kidding me?"

"Ma'am..."

"You seriously want me to pay you fifteen goddamn dollars for some disgusting fried shit for this fat ass that'll see him dead within a year?" She grabbed the man's huge neck, the way a poacher might a dead piece of game. "Look at him!"

"Do you want me to just cancel your order?"

The woman glared. Her husband's red face turned redder. Behind him a family of four, two young kids, were eyeing the couple miserably. "It ain't that much," Wode blurted, unexpectedly, turning to his wife with a kind of fearful anger, "less'n you spend on that damn cat!"

She turned, "What?"

"Fucker's sixteen for Christ sake! That's like goddamn ninety years old! Tut you're still buying him goddamn sweaters and shit and all I want is somethin' to eat for the--"

"Pardon me," Luby began, "sir...ma'am...other people are waiting."

"Shush!" Mrs. Wode turned to her husband, her eyes tearful, "You bastard! Say that again and I'll--"

"You'll do what? Set your damn cat on me?"

"Cotton burger."

The voice behind, its sudden emergence of the heavily accented calm behind where Luby stood jolted her in surprise and silenced the bickering couple. There, Camberline was holding one of the Styrofoam trays, her wrinkled face locked in a wide smile as she plopped it gently on the counter in front of Wode whose eyes almost fell from his skull in astonishment. Astonishment and hunger. Luby could hardly blame him for the former, at least. The cotton burger was a particularly odd creation; a gruesome creation that smelled almost as bad as it looked...and it looked like sweet hell.

Sweet, sweet hell.

It was no true burger at all, of course, but two deep-fried Krispy-Kreme glazed donuts with sprinkles that were pinned with skewers to a 'patty', and the patty was the true genius. Ground meat mixed with cotton-candy, the latter balled tight like loft insulation, engulfing the tiny quantity of flesh. Then, the whole thing was dipped in a coat of batter and fried for just thirty seconds, long enough to turn crispy (although the raw ground beef remained bloody) but short enough so that it would not dissolve in the corn oil. The result was a crisp, alien object. A thing that looked, Luby thought, like a radioactive tumor more than any kind of food. The smell was an over-sweet, caramelized stink that was not unlike the smell of rotting flesh. Mixed with the savory grease of two slices of processed cheese with ketchup, mustard and a slice of bacon, it made her stomach churn. Even years after Pappa had first proudly shown her it, she had never got used to it. A lot of the food FRIED OPEN PLAIN sold she felt that way about. Most of it.

The fat man, however, looked like a kid on Christmas Day.

"Let's go, Wode."

Before Luby could react, the woman had snatched the cotton burger on its Styrofoam tray up and turned and the two of them vanished into the crowd. She watched them leave, sliding her hand into her pocket to take out sixteen dollars from yesterday's pay to give to the drawer, her lips mumbling a greeting to the family who had been waiting. She took their order in silence. Behind, she could feel Camberline lingering. Her wrinkled old face watching her.

By nightfall the fairground was quiet but for the distant rattle-rattle of small change being emptied and counted and occasionally a trash truck making its rounds. Occasionally there were the sparse murmurings of chatter and occasional clicks of distant laughter. Small disturbances that passed across air wounded by agitated pollen, rotting food, and a thousand different smoldering generators.

Mostly, though, all was quiet. As noisy as the fair was by day, it was like a graveyard by night as the place of a million sensory explosions became a dead zone.

Except for the smell.

What came from the fryer had infested every one of Luby's memories for the past nineteen and a half years, infusing each with an unending concoction of rich and vile odors. It was a smell she could not wash off, no matter how many bars of soap she scraped across her skin. Grease from hundreds of forgotten orders danced from the dimly lit kitchen – the place behind the partition where Pappa spent his days.

Deep Fried by George Alan Bradley

Now she could hear him.

He was hard at work as usual, brushing up the remnants of gristle and batter and crumbs that had fallen to the tile. The remains of donut burgers and Twinkie sundaes and M&M nuggets and Fried Smore dumplings and Pas special 'Funnel Cake 'N' Steak Surprise' and all the other things FRIED OPEN PLAIN served up. The smells moved through Luby's brain as if in some conga line as she labored through counting the money in the till.

"Finish?"

The heavy accent again – the word was spoken with exaggerated vowels: *Feeneesh?*

Luby turned her head. There, shrouded by the electric bulbs, Camberline stood, small and elfin over by a sagging sack of trash. In the light her face was the color of French mustard and even more haggard than usual. Luby stared at her, surprised. Not by the question, but more the mere fact Camberline was talking to her at all. In the three weeks since they had hired the old lady on, she could not remember her beginning a single conversation.

"I wish," Luby said, smiling politely.

Camberline came closer, eyeing the register curiously, as though it was some foreign object. Luby wondered if she was going to offer to help. She hoped not. For one thing, Pappa would not allow outsiders to touch his cash. Even old ladies. For another thing, Luby doubted she would be any real help. If anything, she would probably slow the whole thing up.

"No?"

Luby shook her head. "But there's not much more, really. Just need to...check my figures. Few minutes maybe, if that." She rubbed her eyes with her other hand. "How about you, Camberline? Cleaning done?"

She thought that would be enough. If there was one thing she thought she knew about the old woman it was that she hated anybody offering to help her clean anything. But, to her surprise, the old woman didn't move.

"Me se," she said, stepping closer. Suddenly she reached up and, to Luby's surprise, drew her long, brown fingernail in a gentle stroke across Luby's cheek. "Na biandola dandencar. Pe ca?"

Luby stared, surprised. "Huh?"

"You do not speak, chavorro?"

Somewhere in the back she could hear the industrious scrape of Pappa still grinding free the burned rinds of whatever had scalded the grill top. *Poor Camberline,* she remembered Pappa saying, *she's had such a difficult life, Lubela. She wasn't like us, she had to escape the old lands herself. She's a good person, hard working--*

"Ah, I'm a little rusty," Luby said, blushing, "more than a little rusty, actually."

"Rust?" Camberline repeated. "What rust?"

"Out of practice, I mean. My father, he doesn't speak Romani much." She paused. "Not many people around here do, you know? I've never met any."

"Yes." The woman nodded gravely. "This I know."

"Yeah. Well, I better get this done."

Luby turned away, her head beginning to hurt. Truth be told, she didn't feel comfortable around Camberline, and felt increasingly less comfortable the longer she was there. In the past, she had always gotten along okay with the seasonal help. Valentina, the Mexican girl Pappa had hired last summer, had been a good friend. So had Jose, an older man with kind eyes who had taught her to play the harmonica. All of them she had liked for one reason or another. But Camberline was this year's choice and Pappa had not mentioned how he had found her or where; only that one day he had brought her into their motorhome and told Luby she would be working with them for the season. Had she been a little younger, Luby could have understood (Pappa was a man, after all, and Mamma had been dead since she was a toddler) but this was nothing like that. This old woman, whose exact age Luby did not know but she had to be almost seventy, had just materialized somewhere between Marla, Texas and Oklahoma City and had accompanied FRIED OPEN PLAIN from the Tulsa-Newitt rodeo to the state fair in Hutchinson, Kansas, by way of the Hewell County Strawberry Festival. She thought perhaps what made her uncomfortable was the very thing that shouldn't: Because she was a Roma, just like Pappa and she was, technically at least. Luby had met few Roma in her life, there weren't many in Oklahoma, Texas or Kansas, and there was something about that fact which seemed to make a difference. Why, she could not say.

"Can you try speak?" Camberline asked, gently, "maybe our sayings? Or songs?"

Guiltily, Luby looked down at the cash, where in the dark Andrew Jackson regarded her cautiously. "No," she admitted, "not really. I'd like to learn someday, of course."

"Learn," Camberline repeated, sighing pitifully. "As a grown woman?

Learn Romani?"

Luby shrugged. "Like I said, I'm just rusty....my dad, he did teach me some things when I was a kid." She considered this. "I know how to count to ten, I think..."

But the old woman wasn't listening. Instead, she was staring out at the darkened fairground, her mouth twisted in disgust like some old Puritan as she surveyed the empty stalls, the garbage that littered the grass. "It's true what they say, what they warn."

"Excuse me?"

"The Calusari." Camberline regarded her, the smirk vanishing, becoming disappointment. "You do not know of this either, chavarro?"

Luby shook her head blankly.

"But you are a grown woman!"

Luby felt her face reddening, like the way Wode's had. Something about the question, the disappointment, filled her with irrational guilt. "He might have, what is it? The Calusari?"

Camberline was shaking her head. "A true Roma woman would know this, one with the blood."

"I have the blood."

"Yes, you have." She snorted contemptuously. "But what else? No respect, this much I know, no interest."

"Excuse me?" Luby felt a sudden twist of indignation. "The only reason I don't know that stuff is because nobody told me!"

"This I know." The old woman smiled in the yellow light. "But they will not care for your excuses."

"Who won't? What are you even talking about?"

"The Calusari." Her wrinkled eyes widened. Even in the yellow light, she seemed to pale slightly. "The guardians of our blood, they are watching. They are unhappy. This is why they send me, see? I try to give you last chance. You and he." She nodded at the kitchen.

"I don't understand what you're saying?"

"Na biandola dandencar - the child is not born with teeth." Camberline's lip trembled slightly. "These old wisdoms of our people, your people, so you claim. But your father, he did wrong for not teaching, you know this?"

Luby shrugged.

"How about this one? O shoshoy kaste si feri yek khiv sigo athadjol, O..."

Luby shook her head slowly, pretending to count the modest pile of quarters, clicking them back into the till at a rate that was too fast, that she knew made her discomfort obvious.

"You do not know?"

"Nope."

"The rabbit which has only one hole...soon is caught."

"Gotcha." She scooped quarters from the register's inner tray. "Listen, Camberline, I'm gonna finish up here and go back to bed, okay? I'm tired."

"But you say you will learn!"

"Honestly, I was just being polite. I'm not all that interested."

The old woman stared, distraught in a way that no longer troubled Luby but began to amuse her. She wished Pappa would come out, and briefly thought to go find him, anything to get away from this tiresome old hag, but that seemed a silly response. A childish one. She was nineteen, for Christ sake. The woman was a pain in the ass. Probably insane, too.

"Chavarro please..."

"My name's Luby, okay? Now go away, okay? I'm not interested. Too damn tired."

And then Luby heard the music.

Coming from the kitchen, one of the old folk songs with its sinewy fiddle and howling vocals. For a moment she couldn't figure out where it was coming from, then remembered Pappa had a cassette radio back there. Usually when he played music it was the Rolling Stones or Billy Joel or some other dad-age classic rock. But occasionally he would play the traditional music. She remembered hearing it before, anyway.

Our culture, he would say, over and over, *we must sustain it, Luby. At all costs.*

Luby knew there was a part of Pappa that felt guilt about the slow fading of what he called 'our culture'. In fact, she knew he had forgotten most of it in the years since he and Mamma had arrived in Chicago the year before she was born. She knew he cared little for the Roma stuff. He seldom played those old songs and when he did, he would never sing nor tap along to the beat on the stainless steel. For the same reasons she supposed he had hired Camberline, it was nothing more than a token gesture born of guilt. And now that token gesture was going to bug the hell out of her.

"Ajsi bori lachi..."

Luby jolted. Camberline's hand had taken hold of her hand, which still held a fistful of uncounted dimes, and was gripping it so hard it almost hurt.

"...xal bilondo," she muttered, "phenel londo..."

Deep Fried by George Alan Bradley

The dimes spilled, the zinc glistened in the flicker of neon across the thoroughfare, from some High Striker machine the operator had either forgotten about or simply decided to let wear out its battery. Behind, in the kitchen, Pappa's song was replaced instead by a single fiddle accompanied by the clopping of soft jangling tambourine.

"You know this one, chavarro? It is very famous. Back home. In our old home. I'm sure you know it, yes?" Camberline exhaled hopefully. "If you think, yes? All Roma women know this song I believe. It is a love song."

"Nope. I don't."

Camberline's face, she realized, was no longer there. It was a shadow. She looked up, startled, only now realizing the lights that hung about the counter had darkened down to a feeble glower and were barely emitting any light at all.

Meanwhile the light in Pappa's kitchen had gone completely.

It was pitch black.

Where did he go?

"Chavarro?"

Inside of it she could hear, or thought she could, the light tapping of fingers to the tambourine. She looked back at Camberline. "Did you see where he went? My father..."

"There isn't much time, Chavarro! The Calusari. If you do not wish to end up as he."

"What?!"

"He's dead, chavarro."

"Shut up!" Panic lunged in her chest. "Pappa?" she blurted, eyes fixed to the deep black hole where the kitchen had been, her voice quivering, "Pappa! Answer me!'"

"Shh-shh." Camberline's brown nail grazed her cheek. Slower, but harder, digging in. "Kay zhala I suv shay zhala wi o thav...where the needle goes, the thread shall follow." She reached out her yellowed finger, pointing it menacingly, her rotting teeth appearing as she began to smile widely. "It is too late. You're next."

Luby opened her mouth.

"Shh-shh."

There was a sharp crackling. A second later the rest of the lights went out. In the dark, Luby felt something pressed to her throat. Something thin and cold. Something that drained away the scream that came.

"I'll take one of 'em elephant ears..."

She clicked the buttons. An easy job it was, just clicking buttons.

"Two dollars."

The fat man reached for his pocket and then stopped, frowning. He leaned in, almost whispering. "Wasn't it a dollar fifty yesterday?"

"Oh, you're right." She nodded, smiling. Not knowing how to take the item off, she typed it again. "One dollar...fifty."

The man looked pleased. "Sorry," he mumbled, "don't usually care... it's just I promised my wife I wouldn't spend so much money today. She doesn't want me overeating, see?"

"Certainly," she replied, smiling, "anything else for you?"

"Big soda too," the man said, rubbing his mouth with his fleshy forearm. "Diet Pepsi."

"Anything else?"

The man shook his reddish head slowly, while his eyes stroked the words on the wall. His brow began to furrow in intrigue. "What's that there?"

She turned.

"Right there...I...I...can't say its name?"

She didn't look. Didn't need to. It was a popular choice already. Several had been sold just since that morning. "Delicious," she said, holding her smile.

"But what is it?"

"Meat." She flicked her eyelashes flirtatiously. There was no guilt. She had done nothing to render guilt. It had been their direction. Such things were meant to be. "It tastes just like a steak. Only deep fried. Tender and thick and with all the juice. Three dollars."

"Three bucks? That's it?"

"Yessir." She clicked in the price. "Anything else you want?"

"Nope," he said, the salivation growing, oozing from his lips as he handed over a twenty-dollar bill. "Nope, that'll do me fine."

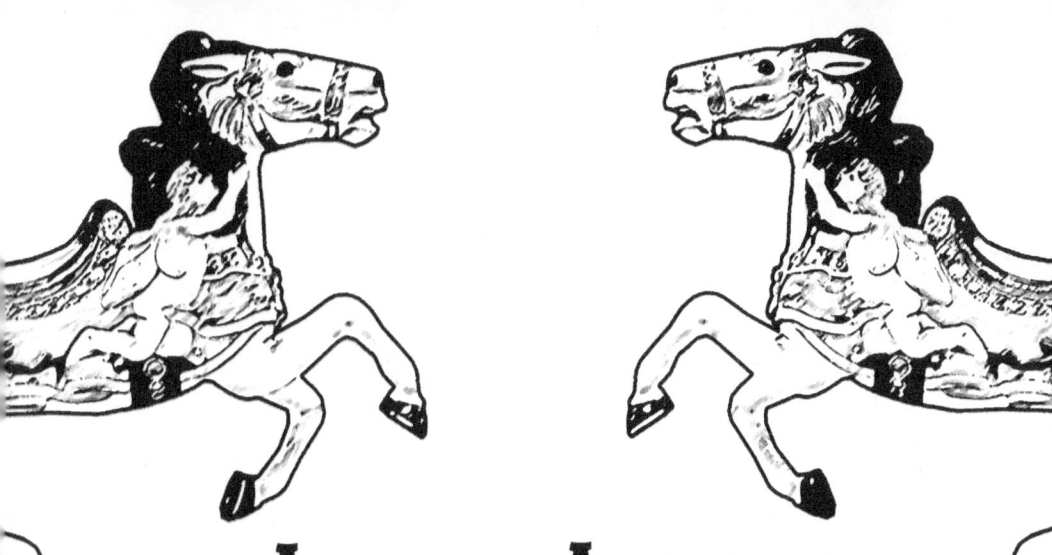

ABOUT THE AUTHOR

Midwest author born in London, George Alan Bradley's writing inhabits a similarly nomadic literary geography. With stories inspired by a broad spectrum of science fiction, suspense, fantasy, and horror, the world of George's writing is one of dark shapes, distressed landscapes, and sharp objects. It is a world in which ordinary people find themselves confronted by monsters both real and imaginary. George lives in Ohio with his wife, Lisa, son Everett and daughter, Evelyn, and a menagerie of peculiar pets. He is currently working on a debut novel while continuing to publish short fiction. WWW.GEORGEALANBRADLEY.COM.

Tami and the Fried Pickle Caper

Chrissy Moon

The Beautiful Tami was here somewhere. I could feel it.

She brought the sun with her wherever she went. That's precisely how she made me feel with those little smiles and greetings when I saw her at school.

But forget school. She was here, at this Carnival of Morning. And I was going to find her.

"Without you I'm empty / so, so dark…"

The newest pop song from that Justin guy was barely audible over the crowd of people. I stopped, straining to listen to the words as a gaggle of little kids nearly ran me over. I yelped amid their apparent determination to get to the Ferris wheel before anybody else. Only with a little bit of luck was I able to keep my balance and remain standing after the herd had passed through me.

"Brian Perry?"

I gasped, not because someone had said my name, but because there was no mistaking the unique, musical voice. Or the way hearing it

116

made me feel.

I planted a smile on my face before turning around, silently praying she didn't hear my gasp. There stood The Beautiful Tami and as expected, the sun was shining behind her. She was one in a million, stunning because of her spirit and the way she carried herself. She was petite and had a perfect face with an adorable little nose. Her straight dark hair reached a little bit past her chin and ended there, not a strand out of place.

"Hey, Spaal." I scrunched up my face.

What? What did that even mean?

I closed my eyes and opened them. One side of her mouth was upturned in a sly smile.

Let's try again, idiot. Take a deep breath.

"Tami!" I smiled at her.

She nodded in approval. "Yes, *that's* my name. Right. I was worried you might've forgotten it there for a second."

"I never forget the name of a beautiful woman."

Whoa! Did I just say that? I am a stud. I am a battle master.

A tint of pink flushed her cheeks, so subtle and so briefly, I halfway wondered if I'd imagined it. No matter. I would always believe she blushed furiously. That's the way to do it.

After a couple seconds, she giggled. It was the cutest sound I've ever heard in my life. I wanted to memorize it. "You're such a smooth talker!" She took a step toward me, arms open.

My mouth dropped open and I panicked. What was going to happen here?

Did you remember to put deodorant on this morning, Brian? DIDJA?

I vaguely remembered doing so this morning. Thank God.

She stood on her toes and put her arms around my neck, leaning in. I laughed – at least, I hoped I did and that I didn't shout, "HORP, HORP!" like a deranged seal. I *like* to think that I chuckled sexily and that she was mesmerized by my smoothness.

And then I made the mistake of breathing in through my nose.

The way she smelled.

I couldn't describe it, but I have never smelled anything so fresh or angelic. I wanted to hold onto her as long as I could. I wanted to...to...

Uh oh.

She smelled *too* good and now there were forces out that were beyond my control. Flustered, I let go of her quickly. I took my backpack off my shoulders and turned it around, holding it in front of me. Making sure that it covered the important areas, I unzipped the backpack and pretended to look through it.

That beautiful scent... it lingered in my nostrils.

Argh!

I found a nearby bench and sat down, placing the bag *carefully* in my lap.

"Hey. Um, everything okay?" Thankfully, The Beautiful Tami looked genuinely confused and as if she had no idea what 'romantic' thoughts I was entertaining, for which I was eternally grateful. I kept fiddling with the contents in my bag for her sake.

"Oh, yeah, I, uh...I'm just, well, looking for my phone. Where is it?!"

I waited until she looked away from me before I secretly took my phone from out my jeans pocket and threw it into my bag. I then made a big show of 'finding' it while she turned back around.

She smiled. My heart flipped while thankfully, a different body part went back to normal and I was once again free to interact with the opposite sex.

"Brian, I absolutely HAVE to try their fried pickles, or I'll never forgive myself." She paused for a few seconds and added, "Do you wanna come with? You can have some."

Need I mention how adorable she was for offering to share her snack with me?

I gazed at her, realizing after a moment that my mouth was hanging open. I closed it, cleared my throat and nodded, which was silly because she wasn't looking anywhere near me; she was already headed to the food stands. "Yasso!" I shouted after her.

What did I say?

Hopefully, she didn't hear my nonsense as the carnival was getting pretty crowded with kids and adults alike. I wasn't going to lose this golden opportunity to spend time with her. I really did like her, even if her idea of the perfect snack was *fried pickles.*

No one's perfect, Brian, I told myself.

So, I was forced to eat a slice of fried pickle. It took every ounce of strength I could muster to only heave and gag on the *inside.* It tasted awful and pretty much resembled everything I hated about the human race. But I chewed and smiled, chewed and smiled.

She was worth it. She would always be worth it.

I continued on, even when my intestines began garbling in really uncomfortable ways.

If I ignore it, it'll go away.

That was the solution to *all* problems.

A small stabbing pain hit me, followed with more churning sensations.

Soon, I could barely hang onto The Beautiful Tami's words as my entire consciousness was focused on preventing my butt from exploding.

This is why I don't eat deep-fried food, people.

To make matters worse, Tami began taking off her jacket. I would have loved to enjoy this visual moment, but my tumbling insides were winning the battle. And then, like the angel that she was, she saved me.

"I'm just going to put my jacket in the car. Can you hold the food for a minute? I'll be right back."

I smiled and nodded. Secretly, I was also clenching my butt muscles and really trying not to think about how she just referred to this platter of atrocity as *food*.

She'd only taken a single step when her phone rang. She sighed and glanced over her shoulder at me, the single most adorable thing I have ever seen a girl do. She smiled apologetically before answering the call.

"Hey, Dad...what? No, I'm...Of course I'm coming home soon, I'm just out with a friend..."

She gestured to me while she said that last part, as if her Dad could see that.

I tried not to read too much into it. Was I the reason she was at this carnival? Just like *she* was the reason for *me* being at the carnival, as well as my reason for going to school every day?

Maybe?

"I...ugh. Will you relax? I know we had talked about visiting Grandma today, but I thought I could just go to the carnival really quick and come back...and I thought we might see her *next* weekend..." She trailed off, rolled her eyes, and sighed. She lowered her phone so it was away from her face and locked eyes with me, saying, "Sorry, Brian, I...I gotta go." Then she turned and walked away, putting her phone back to her ear. I could hear her dad's raised voice from where I was.

Gotta go? Meaning, I wouldn't see her until tomorrow?

Demonic Carnival

I could have sworn that with every step she took toward the parking lot, the more dismal the entire carnival seemed to get. My insides garbled in agreement, reminding me of my unfortunate digestive predicament.

Right. My clenching butt.

The exact millisecond that The Beautiful Tami was out of sight, I made a beeline for the row of porta-potties, chucking the fried pickles into the first trash bin that I saw.

I love you, Tami, but I can't take these where I'm going.

I ducked into a potty stall and let loose. Whoever would come in after me would not have a fun time here, but that wasn't my problem.

I finished up, grateful that my mom always put some emergency anti-bacterial wipes in my backpack.

Putting my backpack on, I tossed my used wipes into the plastic bucket that passed for a toilet. I opened the porta-potty door and did a double-take at the world outside.

And coiled back, not breathing.

At a loss for words.

This couldn't be right. I looked back inside the toilet for some reason, as if that could tell me anything, and shook my head to myself. This...no. Was I crazy? What was happening? Was I dreaming?

Darkness waited for me outside.

Cold night air kissed my arms.

I walked out cautiously; the carnival bathed in shadows. In the distance, two parking-lot lights provided the only illumination as far as I could see. I stood next to the toilets, waiting for my eyes to adjust. It was so dark.

It was so empty.

Stuffed animals still hung on the walls as prizes offered in game booths. This confused me even more. If I'd somehow fallen asleep on the toilet and this was now the middle of the night, wouldn't everything be put away and the rides all folded up or whatever they did when they were ready to move on to the next town? Not one carnival employee was in sight. Not one guest.

Where were all the *people?*

A creaking sound emanated from somewhere on the grounds, something made from metal like the little door from one of the rides being moved or settling into place.

Movement. Life!

Anxious to find the only other person who survived this mysterious apparent apocalypse, I pushed my fear down and walked briskly toward the source of the noise. Maybe whoever was stuck here with me would know what had happened here.

"Hey!" The sound of my own voice frightened me here in this darkness. "Who's there? Can you tell me what's going on?" I continued walking, determined to find that other person. I didn't get a good feeling from these empty rides I walked past. It felt like invisible people were sitting in the rides watching me, or that somehow the rides *themselves* were checking me out.

When I was little, we lived in a house that was right next to a haunted one. Every time I walked out my front door, I imagined the windows transforming into giant eyes, my every moment being watched. I had that same feeling now, only every carnival attraction was like an open metal coffin, waiting for me.

I never liked the dark. I did my best to avoid it at all times and though everything was barely illuminated by two far-off streetlights, the carnival was so condensed, so packed with booths and rides, that it was swimming in shadows.

And that's when I saw it, standing several booths away. I would never forget it as long as I lived. I know because I've been seeing a therapist for twenty years and I still can't forget this goddamn thing.

It's called a dreever. I know that now. And *how* I knew, I have no idea; I just saw it and knew it. Everything that happened next floated into my brain and took residence there, and I would never be free from it.

It looked like it was made of bones, but it wasn't a skeleton. It was as if someone took random bones from different creatures and glued them together to form a semi-humanoid shape. The bones also looked black, almost as if the creature had been burned, but rather than look brittle, the bones comprised a massive, solid pitch-black shape. It was hard to see in the darkness.

That wasn't the worst part, however. No, that honor belonged to the dreever's head. It almost looked like a huge clear cylinder was rammed halfway into its skull and seemed to be made of the same material as its body. Inside that cylinder was red liquid that sloshed back and forth when the creature moved its head.

I stood there wondering, horrified and curious at the same time. It hadn't noticed me yet; it was busy looking at its arms and legs as if mystified by its own existence. It was moving its body around a little as though it was trying on a new outfit and wanted to determine if it could move around freely in it, but what scared me about this, I mean what *really* scared me, was that its every movement was jerky and disjointed. Even its neck movements as it lowered its head to get a good view of its massive bony arm. It made me think of a robot come to life, every motion predetermined. Except the dreever was sentient. I could feel its curiosity about itself.

"What are you?" I whispered in horror.

It screeched and jerked its head in my direction, its glowing white eyes falling on me.

Run.

It took a slow step towards me, red liquid dripping out of its mouth onto the grass.

Run.

Another step.

Run!

Another. Faster, this time.

RUN, BRIAN!

I yelled at my brain internally until my body obeyed and I stumbled away in the other direction, with no immediate plan in mind except to put as much distance between the dreever and me as possible.

I ran toward the porta-potty without really thinking about why. Maybe because in my mind, it was my only shelter, the only thing about this Carnival of Nothing that was familiar to me.

The door was closed and I, crouched down on the floor of the plastic booth, awaited my tragic end that closed in on me more every moment.

I didn't expect what happened next.

Silence.

Nothing.

I looked up, unsure, untrusting. Carefully, slowly, I unlocked the door. I pushed it open a little when chaos hit the porta-potty, the dreever climbing up the booth like a gigantic spider and sitting directly on top of it. I could see its dark mass above me.

My heart pounded. Maybe I could run back out and it wouldn't catch me in time?

I opened the door again; one of the dreever's long appendages hit me, disorienting me for a moment. It was so big that it could sit on top of the porta potty and dangle an arm across the front of it at the same time.

Tami and the Fried Pickle Caper by Chrissy Moon

The dreever jumped back on the ground and yanked me out, hurling me face-first onto the grass outside. It followed me and swiftly closed its arms around me.

I trembled as it put its hand close to my face, the sharp claw on one of its fingers barely glinting in the dim light. I yelled in agony as a hot burst of pain pinched the area above my right ear. I felt my skin getting sliced open, my head warm and wet. I was sprawled out on the grass, the dreever there above me now, still meddling with my head.

I was losing my battle with the dreever.

With darkness.

One eye got blurry from blood seeping into it. Everything hurt then, and as I felt myself slowly fade away into nothing, slowly to become part of this Carnival of Nothing, I watched the moon with my other eye.

And then the soft glow surrounding the moonlight began to flow into a shadow of its own, thickening until it was like an iridescent plush cloud, traveling closer, getting bigger.

The dreever noticed it too and moved back, shrieking at the cloud in great annoyance.

I blinked and opened my eyes again, though with great difficulty. The dreever had backed up even more and was by the porta-potty, watching me closely. The moon cloud wrapped itself around my arm and felt warm.

It felt like life.

The cloud became smooth and almost felt like a…hand.

"Brian! Hey!"

But that was a voice I knew. A voice that could sing with angels.

I saw her. Moon glow fading, a human materializing.

The human.

The Beautiful Tami.

"Wha…"

Tried to open my eyes all the way. Didn't have the strength. Closed them, then opened them, and if I had not already been lying on the ground, I would have fallen over with relief in seeing Tami's hand wrapped around my arm. She was stooped on the ground beside me, her face hovering over me, her eyes searching mine, her other hand gently shaking me awake.

"Tami…" I muttered.

Close, open.

The food booth behind her began to fix itself, the little glass windows smooth once more and the painted signs on the side bright. I could even hear someone else's voice now, in the distance, the vendor inside the booth selling food to the customers.

Customers...

A little girl and her mother walked past us. Under the child's arm was a stuffed animal that happily played "You Are My Sunshine."

And then another person walking around.

And then another.

Then, the same gaggle of little kids from before, racing back from the Ferris wheel, stumbling over me.

Off in the distance, the Ferris wheel coming into motion like a train, slowly turning once again.

Close, open.

The dreever had been watching me, red liquid dripping from its mouth to the ground.

It watched me, tilting its head from side to side with its jerky movements until it faded away for good.

The sky became bright once more, as if it were always there, making me question my sanity.

No more lightheadedness. My hand flew up to my ear.

The wound was gone.

What the hell?

"Brian, why are you on the ground? Did you pass out? Are you okay?"

"Tami," I said, more aware this time.

More grateful.

I hadn't been dreaming. As I looked into The Beautiful Tami's eyes, the Tunnel of Love changed from being abandoned and broken into a clean, operable ride once again. I even took my eyes off her for a moment so I could fully appreciate it repairing itself, an event that no one else around me seemed to notice at all.

She turned to see where I was looking.

"Hey, great idea!" she said brightly. The cutest giggle anyone has ever heard lit up my life. "Let's go together."

She wants to go to the Tunnel of Love with me. ME, the battle master himself.

"Wait. I thought you left." I said that last part with an inflection, so it sounded like a question.

"Well, yeah. I was going to. I'm sorry about that. My dad had wanted me to come home, but I finally convinced him he could wait a little longer."

Tami and the Fried Pickle Caper by Chrissy Moon

I looked at her mouth. I so wanted to kiss it.

She was still holding onto my arm, so as she moved to sit next to me on the grass, I took my other hand and touched her face. She leaned her head into my touch, which was a moment I would remember forever.

"Where are the pickles?" she asked me suddenly.

Oh no! The fried pickles. *The ones I threw out.* It all started coming back to me.

I could feel my face getting hot. I wanted to be honest with her, but how could I tell her that I threw them in the trash because my butt needed to explode?

I must have had a look of terror on my face because she giggled. "Oh, that's okay, Brian. I'm not mad at you for finishing the pickles. I didn't know you liked it *that much!* Hey, I have a great idea. Before we go in the Tunnel of Love, let's get two more plates of pickles so we don't have to share. Come on!"

She smiled sweetly and yanked me back to the food stands. I could have, should have run, but *she was touching me now.* We were just one step away from kissing and cuddling, and like I said earlier, she would always be worth it.

As she dragged me away, I looked back at the porta-potty with exhausted trepidation.

"I'll see you again real soon," I said quietly to it.

The porta-potty door flapped in response.

ABOUT THE AUTHOR

Don't be fooled by Chrissy Moon's friendly demeanor. Inside, she's a tornado of unwritten psychological thrillers and iced dark chocolate latte dreams. Who isn't, right?

She loves languages, has no drawing talent whatsoever, and celebrates every Summerween with her two sons.

Want to get in touch with her? Find her at:
Instagram: https://instagram.com/chrissymoonauthor/
Twitter: https://twitter.com/WriterAngel
FB: https://www.facebook.com/AuthorChrissyMoon/
Official site: www.chrissymoon.com

Be Nice

A.E. Santana

Ivette sensed the carnival before pulling the car into the dirt lot. Carousal music mingled with shouts of glee. The scents of fried food, smoked meats, and sugary treats wafted through the air. Ivette's friends, rambunctious twins Regina and Priscilla, had almost not been allowed to go with her, but Ivette's reputation of being the sweet, polite friend swayed their parents.

The dirt parking lot was sparsely sprinkled with vehicles. Ivette was torn on how she felt about that. On one hand, there would be smaller lines for rides. On the other hand, it made for lousy boy hunting, and at seventeen that was important.

The carnival was styled as a vintage 1920s circus with antiqued music and décor. The staff was dressed in old-fashioned apparel and spoke in heightened "old-timey" talk. It would have been silly and amusing if it wasn't for the repeated motif of little red devils.

Ivette frowned. Something was *off*. Something more than just the bizarre dedication to the little red man. The carousel music cranked over the rusty speakers with a tinny undertone; and underneath that, Ivette heard something else: a strange chant that slipped into the shouts of the barkers and beneath the beeps, zaps, and hums of the games and rides. She strained to hear the word, but the more she tried to catch it, the more it sounded like gibberish: *as...mo...dey....*

"What's up?" Regina asked. Ivette had fallen behind the twins. She didn't answer right away, unsure of what to say and from the fear of bringing down the mood or, worse, sounding like a weird-o.

"I'm fine," Ivette said.

Priscilla tossed another piece of popcorn in her mouth. "Good, because we're about to go on whatever's fastest."

"Hey, sweetie!" A lewd voice called out. A carnival performer, who must have been on stilts because he towered over the crowd, eyed Ivette. He wore a bizarre outfit of black and red, mimicking scales and claws. His painted face twisted in a grotesque grin, and horns jutted out from a faux exposed skull. "Girlie!" He called again and pointed a gross black nail at Ivette. "Devil got your tongue?"

Ivette, caught off guard, stared blankly.

"That's good," the performer said. He bent low and leered at her: "I like 'em quiet."

Ivette squirmed, unexpectedly troubled by the carnival worker's comment. *It's fine*, she thought. *This is his job.* But she felt uncomfortable. The shouts and laughter from the carnival rides suddenly seemed more like nervous and frightened screams.

"Hey!" Priscilla shouted back. "Do you like them wet?" Then she flung her supersized soda at the performer, hitting him in the face. The carnival worker squawked and staggered, running into a booth and knocking displays to the ground. Half the crowd laughed while the other half murmured in disapproval.

Ivette gasped. Shamefaced, she grabbed the twins and hurried away from the scene. "What is your problem?" she asked as they moved out of sight.

"You can't let that thing talk to you like that," Regina said.

Priscilla nodded. "My drink was sacrificed for your honor."

Humiliation and anger seared through Ivette, but she didn't want to be the party-pooper. She took a deep breath. "I'm okay," she said. "I just don't want to get in trouble."

"That guy was a jerk and a half," Priscilla said.

Around the corner, before the midway opened up, a platform with a large metal structure sat off to the side. "Hey," Ivette said. "Let's try the simulator?" She wanted to smooth things over with the twins, show them she was still game.

Regina gave it a once over. "Waste tickets on that thing?" she asked. "I'd rather stand in line for the port-o-potties."

Be Nice by A.E. Santana

"But there is no line there," Ivette said.

"That should be your first clue," Priscilla said. But they drifted toward the structure: a peculiar boxy configuration, devoid of any signage, that sat on a makeshift steel platform. "Where's the carny?" Priscilla asked.

"Don't say 'carny,'" Ivette said.

"Hello!" Priscilla called out. "Carny!"

There was a click, and the side of the structure slid open. A young man stepped out. His handsome face was splashed with freckles and his green eyes shone brightly, a compliment to the shock of red hair waving around his ears. He was tall with broad shoulders and a fit physic underneath his vintage carnival barker's outfit.

He smiled and Ivette's knees wobbled. The sour pit in her stomach fluttered. Maybe the other carnival worker was a jerk, but this young man was all chivalry and charm. She wanted things to go back to normal, so she smiled. *Nothing had really happened anyway*, Ivette told herself. The twins shared an annoyed look.

Regina muttered: "I guess we're getting on this ride."

Priscilla whispered jokingly into Ivette's ear: "A carny, Ivette? A carny? Have we learned nothing?"

"A redheaded carny," Regina said.

"He looks like Carrot Top's rejected clone," Priscilla said.

"Carrot Top looks like Carrot Top's rejected clone," Regina said. "This guy is Carrot Top's rejected test tube baby."

"He is not!" Ivette said. "And shut up." But she was glad they were on good terms again.

Regina moved ahead of her friends and stopped at the platform steps. "How many tickets to ride this jalopy?"

"Two tickets each," the carnival worker said with a thick Southern accent. Ivette's knees went weak.

"Two?" Priscilla complained. "Look here, carny—"

"Two is fine," Ivette said, cutting Priscilla off and rushing forward. "I got it." She dug around in her bag for the tickets. When she looked up, the carnival worker was gazing down at her. The butterflies in her stomach swooned. She walked up the steps to hand him the tickets. For a moment, he only stared at her—his green eyes devastatingly beautiful.

"Good choice," he finally said, and plucked the tickets from her hand.

Ivette shrugged and chuckled awkwardly. "Sorry about them," she said about the twins.

"No worries, darlin'," he said and winked. "It's nice to be appreciated. Not many folks come by this ride." He smiled. Ivette felt her breath leave her. Spellbound—is that what she was feeling?

"Get a room!" Priscilla called out.

"What's your name?" the carnival worker asked, ignoring the twins' heckles.

"Ivette."

"I'm Caleb." He stepped aside and tipped his hat to her.

"Don't," Priscilla said as the twins stepped up. "You're going to give her 'the vapors.'"

Regina peeked inside the cab. It was dark and smelled. "So...the theme's garbage truck?"

"Dad's van," Priscilla said.

"No theme," Caleb said. "You'll go where your desire leads you."

Priscilla elbowed Ivette. "Is this going to take you to Caleb's bedroom?"

Ivette scowled. "It's going to take me to jail for murdering you."

"Keep hold of your desires and wishes," Caleb said. He held up the six tickets, fanned out for effect. "Please, enter."

The twins made room for Ivette to sit up front with them. The strange smell penetrated the air, fetid and spoiled. A large screen blinked on and the door slid shut, leaving the girls in the dim light of the simulator screen. There was a hum, and below the hum: as...mo...dey...

The screen shimmered and a tunnel appeared before them. The tunnel spun, creating a whirlpool effect. "What do you see?" Ivette asked.

"Nothing," one twin replied. "Everything," the other said. Both their words were labored breathy whispers.

In the middle of the swirl, a hazy red dot appeared. The smell in the ride rose to an overpowering stench. The hum grew louder, and the seats began to shift. The red pinprick glowed and expanded—whatever was at the end of the tunnel was moving towards them. Ivette's skin went moist with sweat and her eyes stung with it. Was it a fire rushing toward her and her friends? Or maybe, they were falling. Yes, she felt the seats shift again. They were falling and a fire was heading for them. Her muscles jerked underneath her skin, but her body didn't move—couldn't. She didn't scream. The twins didn't scream. She felt out of control, hypnotized. Why couldn't she scream?

As the red dot and the girls approached each other, Ivette realized it wasn't fire. It was Caleb. He walked towards them, his red hair a beautiful, bright target. He seemed to emerge from the screen.

The ride stopped.

Ivette found control over her body and quickly turned to her friends. But she was sitting alone, the inside of the simulator suddenly vast. Panic dug deep into her.

Caleb bowed and extended his hand out to Ivette. She hesitated. *What the hell is happening?* But another thought—alien, slick, and shiny—barreled its way to the front of her mind: *Don't make a fuss.* She took Caleb's hand, and he helped her to her feet.

What is going on? Ivette wanted to ask. Instead she smiled and said, "I can't wait." *What?* She didn't mean to say that. Alarm swarmed inside her. *Where are my friends?* Her brain asked. But she said, "I've waited so long." Ivette stiffened, and Caleb's grip on her hand tightened.

"Not long now," he said.

Ivette felt her lips twist into a crazy smile. "I'm so glad," she heard her voice say. Caleb gripped her elbow, pulling her closer as they stepped up to the vortex. The smell of rotten eggs and rot assaulted her. She wanted to reel back from it, instead she allowed Caleb to put his arm around her shoulder.

Get off of me! "This is what I want." *I don't know what's happening!* "Thank you, Caleb." She knew her face showed no signs of her inner torment; she could feel her dumb smile beaming at the young man—as if she was wearing a mask of complacency.

The air was bloated with rotten odors that choked her brain and lungs, and in it was the agonizing song: mo…deus…as…. There was an ugly, sick sway and Caleb seemed to grow.

I don't want this! Ivette thought. *STOP!*

Caleb's freckled skin morphed as he lengthened. His teeth grew long, and his lips thinned into nothing. The vintage carnival outfit ripped as his body bulged beneath it. Flesh transformed into scales, hair into horns, and hands into talons. There was a horrendous crack and his face split, his skull cracking into three. It re-shaped into different heads: a bull's, huge with flaring nostrils and gnashing teeth; a man's head, grotesque and lecherous; the third looked like a ram, with massive curly horns and angry red eyes.

Ivette stared in disbelief. *This can't be happening*, she thought. *I'll shut my eyes. It'll go away.* But she watched, paralyzed with fear.

"Come along," the human face said. Its lipless mouth grinned, showing dirty fangs. "Be *nice*."

A sharp and achy sorrow, weighted down with shame, descended on Ivette. Was this her fault? She struggled to breath and a buzzing sound deafened her, but in the back of her mind she heard Regina's voice: *You can't let that thing talk to you like that.* She remembered the cool, sticky spray of Priscilla's soda as it collided with the performer's devil face.

Ivette forced her mouth to say what she wanted. "Let. Me. Go." The words squeaked out dry, as if she hadn't talked in years.

The demon stared at her, a look of surprise in its six eyes before it blinked it away. "Nobody likes a girl that speaks out of turn," it said. "What happened to nice Ivette?"

"I..." she struggled out. "Don't have to be—"

"You came here," the demon said. "You want this."

Ivette shook her head. "Don't," she said, forcing the words from her throat. "Talk to me. Like that."

"Aren't I your dream boy?" The man head asked. The ram head said, "You sought me out, so now you're mine." Ivette shook her head. The demon clutched her tighter. "Doesn't matter," said the bull head. "I have you now. I'm bigger than you, stronger than you." The human head opened its large mouth and the stench of sulfur and brimstone seeped out. The monster lifted Ivette into the air, positioning her above its massive face. Its human tongue lashed at her backside, and Ivette squirmed in disgust. She felt helpless, fragile, and stupid. She squeezed her eyes tight.

The demon slipped Ivette into its mouth and she crashed into a crooked tooth. The fang sliced her arm and she heard the demon moan as it tasted her blood. She tried to move away, but the tongue punched her back against the teeth. A gash opened across her back. The demon gurgled her blood, a laugh building in its throat.

It's playing with me, Ivette thought.

The demon swished her around, and she landed flat against one of the teeth. She felt the tooth give in the gum, so she threw her body against it. The creature howled. Ivette hit the tooth again, wedging it free, but she slipped and cut her shoulder on the fang as it tumbled out of the row of razor teeth. The demon tilted its head back and swallowed. Ivette and the tooth slid down the monster's throat.

A chorus of voices leapt up from deep within the monster's belly. The same sing-song word that had followed Ivette through the carnival was so close she finally understood it: Asmodeus. Call it what it is, the voices

Be Nice by A.E. Santana

said. Asmodeus. Demon of Lust. The Tempter. The Defiler. The Rapist. Call it! The choir shouted.

Ivette slammed the fang into the side of the demon's throat, and its scream shook through its esophagus. She pushed back against the other side of the throat, forcing the tooth farther into the flesh. Clutching the fang, hands slick with saliva and blood, she tugged the tooth down until it hacked a hole in the demon's neck. Ivette thrust her head through.

The demon clawed at its neck, trying to squeeze her back in. Ivette screamed, and shoved her foot down on the slit, tearing it wider. She jammed her body through and plunged forward, hitting the floor hard. The demon roared and put its talons to its neck.

Scrunched against the simulator wall, with the demon wailing and lashing out, Ivette searched the room that seemed to be a hundred times larger than before. The large fang she had liberated from the demon's awful mouth lay at its cloven feet. Ivette took a steadying breath before hurling herself toward the tooth. She grabbed it, the demon's hooves nearly crushing her. She yelled up at the demon: "Where are my friends?"

The demon whipped its three heads around and scowled down at her. Carousel music, sped up to a maddening pace, filtered in through the vortex. The three heads spoke all at once: "I have devoured them."

Ivette, blood pooling around her and left arm hanging useless from her shoulder, said, "Look how well that worked for me."

The demon snorted in response and Ivette jumped forward, startling it. She stabbed at the ram's throat and cleaved it open. The edge of the beast's hoof caught Ivette and lifted her in the air. When she landed, there was a bloody slash across her midsection. But she smiled. Tumbling out of the ram's throat was Regina.

Dizzy and pale, Regina stumbled over to her friend. Ivette shoved the large tooth into Regina's hands. "Here," Ivette said, her words moist with the blood in the back of her throat. "Open the bull's neck."

Regina nodded. She took the tooth, then vomited. Still, she was in better shape than Ivette, and rushed the demon. The beast slammed a monstrous claw over her, slashing her leg. Regina yelped, and the demon threw its heads back and laughed. She took the opportunity and plunged the fang into the bull's exposed throat. The demon roared and slapped Regina away, tossing her aside like a ragdoll and leaving the tooth embedded in its flesh.

Regina scrambled to her feet, throwing herself against the fang. She grabbed the tooth and wiggled it into an angle, allowing her to rip the bull's throat open. There was a greasy shredding sound and a howl of rage from the demon. Regina and Ivette shouted in triumph as Priscilla spilled from the bull's throat.

Landing on her face, Priscilla groaned, and blood gushed from her nose. Regina forced her up and hurried them towards Ivette.

"It's Asmodeus," Ivette said, her voice was still weak, but at least the blood had left her throat. "The demon of lust."

"A demon, Ivette?" Priscilla said, blood slathered over her face. "A demon?"

The demon bellowed. Carousel music swelled and deafened the girls. The vortex spun, producing a powerful drag. Ivette lost her footing and felt the twins slip with her. A strange sound, terrifying and *wrong* worked over the carnival music. The demon was laughing. The ragged sound struggled from the holes in its throats and snorted out of its various nostrils and warped mouths.

Priscilla gazed at the monster in disbelief. "Screw that," she said and stood up. "Knock it off, you ugly prick!" Ivette and Regina tried to hold Priscilla back, but she broke away. "Hey! You over compensating with all those heads?" The demon frowned at Priscilla, its faces a mixture of bewilderment and offense. "You look surprised," Priscilla said. "It doesn't help."

The demon screeched and the sound tore at the girls, like millions of tiny knife-footed spiders dancing down into their eardrums.

"Didn't like that?" Priscilla asked, her voice strained with anger. "That's too bad, because I didn't like being swallowed by a B-movie reject!"

Ivette grabbed Priscilla and tugged her down. "Stop," she said. "You're gonna get us killed."

"We're dead anyway," Priscilla said and jumped back up. "Yo! Idiot!"

The demon moved to charge them, but the force from the vortex pulled on it and the monster faltered.

Regina gasped. "More," she said to her sister. She adjusted her grip on the fang and looked at Ivette. "Insults now."

"You...ah..." Ivette said.

Priscilla shouted: "Your birth certificate is an apology letter from the condom factory!"

Ivette struggled to keep her footing but turned to address the beast. "Hey," she said, feeling like her voice was lost as the vortex sucked the air out of the room. Still, the demon turned to her. Ivette's heart pounded and the blood in her mouth tasted metallic. "Hey," she said. "Three-headed moron." She was disturbed by the weakness of her voice; it betrayed the hurt and uncertainty she felt.

The demon laughed and the fragmented sound rippled away into the vortex. "Little girl," the human head said, a whistle of air escaping from the hole in its throat. "You don't mean that, do you?"

"Oh, she means it," Priscilla said, "and if I had any one of your faces, I'd sue my parents."

The demon scowled and took an unstable step towards Ivette and Priscilla. "How dare you!"

Priscilla grinned at the demon. "You must have been born on a highway because that's where most accidents happen."

"You've got stupid red skin," Ivette said. "And dumb horns!"

The comment was lame, but Priscilla laughed. The sound was boisterous, merry, and harsh. Her laughter threw the demon into a frenzy but made Ivette smile. She joined Priscilla, and the girls leaned on each other laughing hysterically, creating aches in their chests and bellies.

"Stop!" The demon bawled. "You little bitches!"

"You—you," Priscilla started to say, but couldn't form the words with the laughter barreling out of her.

"I'll devour—!" The demon began, but its words were replaced with a gag and snarl. Ivette and Priscilla stopped laughing and snapped their heads up to see Regina standing underneath the demon. She had thrust the monster's fang deep into its belly. Blood poured over her. She gritted her teeth and sliced down. The demon moved to attack her but slid backward on its blood.

Horrified and exhilarated, the girls watched as the swirling red hole pulled the demon in. The circus music and the chant of "Asmodeus" were swallowed as the vortex winked out of sight. The door slid open.

Outside, the carnival was in ruins. The rides and booths were destroyed and engulfed in flames. Smoke and screams filled the air. People were chased by demons and other monstrosities. Tired and bloodied, the girls reacted. Panic and survival flight instincts rushed them through the carnival, their eyes and minds closed to the carnage. There was no time to register the pandemonium, their only thought was to get away.

In the car, Ivette sped out of the dirt lot, dust billowing behind them. The twins were uncharacteristically quiet as they let the situation wash over them. In Ivette's mind, images of the carnival in chaos dissolved into

DEMONIC CARNIVAL

Caleb's face. *It wasn't just me*, she thought, and terrible tears of thankfulness slipped down her face.

About the Author

.E. Santana is a Southern California native who writes horror and fantasy. She is the author of several short stories and plays. Her MFA in fiction is from the University of California, Riverside, and she received her bachelor's degree in mass communications with a minor in script writing from California State University, San Bernardino. A.E. Santana is a founding playwright for East Valley Rep. She has quite an affinity for cats. She can be found at www.aesantana.com and on Instagram and Twitter @foxflur.

Tilt-A-Whirl

M.B. Meraki

I always think about the sudden burst of loud calliope music from the movie *The Lost Boys*—"To the Shock of Miss Louise"—when I come to a carnival, followed by a Pavlovian urge for cotton candy and to go for a stomach-churning spin on my all-time favorite ride; the Tilt-A-Whirl. The increasing aroma of powdered sugar on oily dough let me know my best friend Cindy was about to join me as I paid for my sugary snack, from her stop at the fried-dough stand, then we headed to the ruby-colored spinning pods that will make us wonderfully dizzy.

People watching is one of my absolute favorite hobbies to do while trapped anywhere, but carnivals make it especially fun. I like to think up stories about what people's lives are like and sharing this hobby with my friend makes it so much more enjoyable.

Using my pink-fluff-on-a-paper-cone to point at the obviously bored goth girl with her pitch-black hair, kohl eyeliner, and blood-red lips, I said, "She's really having fun, but is in her rebellious phase so has to make it look like she's unhappy that her parents 'dragged' her here. Secretly, though, she's hoping her dad wins her a teddy bear like he always does, he makes her feel loved, even on her darkest days."

"Awww, so sweet!" Cindy said of my 'real-life' story, but quickly chose her own target, turning to point out an overly affectionate couple with a third-wheel trailing behind them, "That third-wheel is secretly in love with *both* of them, but has no idea how to tell them, so stays silent, ever watching and pining a way for them."

It was sad, but probably all too true, "They will notice him and his love for them someday, and they will share his love," I said trying to make it a happier ending then I thought he would likely get.

Scanning over the nearby carnival goers, choosing my next target to make my 'real-life' proclamation, I can't help smirking as I spot my mark. "See business-suit-guy by the Hall-of-Mirrors? See how he's looking expectantly at each person who comes out between looking at his watch? He's not waiting for his family, anxious because its nearly midnight and kids are still out so late. He's really a demon, the personification of Pride, silently judging people as they come out to see who are the vainest, so he can snatch them away and take them to Hell for their sins."

"Absolutely!" Cindy mumbled around the dough in her mouth.

We carried on like that till our snacks were gone, we were at the front of the line, and the rush of 'being next' hit us. Like excited toddlers, we scrambled for the 'perfect car' because it would suck to get a dud that didn't spin well. Once we settled on a car we chose our sides; I sat on the right, she sat on the left, and readied ourselves to battle for control of the car, trying our hardest to lean in 'our direction' to make it spin that way.

The music started when all the cars were filled, and the lap-bars lowered themselves to hold us securely in the seat so we wouldn't fly out while tilting and whirling. Eagerly I tried to catch the eye of our 'tilt-man' and he greeted me with a nod. I gestured toward the control pendant with its three switches; on, off and 'joy'. I spun my finger in the air a few times while giving him a hopeful grin, his return nod and smirk thrilled me. If he was a good tilt-man, he'd be giving us one hell of a ride. By using the brakes on the table we spun on at just the right times while letting the car continue to move freely, giving us some serious g-force spinning action.

Adrenaline kicked in and my heart thundered in my chest as the platform started to turn, then the individual tables and at last the cars themselves. Cindy and I immediately fought for control of the spin—leaning in opposite directions—and cackling with laughter. Soon we were spinning around clockwise, she won the first round, but I knew the tilt-man had my back and we'd be whirling dervishes in no time.

The music was loud and obnoxious, just as it should be, and I started to hear the screams of fellow riders so Cindy and I joined the chorus; the more noise you made, the longer the tilt-man would let you ride for, I learned that when I was a kid riding with my dad, and since that day I have made sure to scream myself hoarse.

When you're spinning around so fast it's hard to see anything more than the blur of the other cars and the world as it all whooshed by, but I thought I saw something in one of the cars that made me feel uneasy, "Cin! Cin! Did you see that?"

"See what?"

That answered that question; she hadn't seen it. As we spun I tried to spot it again. I had no idea what it was, but something was wrong. "Lean this way, we need to slow down!" I demanded so I could try to get a better view of whatever it was I had barely glanced at in my peripheral.

"No way! I'm winning!" Cindy crowed because we were spinning in 'her direction'.

Surely if there were something wrong the tilt-man would see it too and stop the ride, but we were speeding up, so I tried to put it out of my mind and just enjoy myself.

As normally happens on the Tilt-A-Whirl ride, the car slowed its spinning and finally paused at the peak of its swing, the joy button had been hit! Our table was stopped, but the car was still loose. We were on the highest part of the platform, the car was ready to change directions, and it gave me mere seconds where I could see some other cars clearly now.

What I saw made my heart drop into my stomach.

A father and two kids we had skipped in our 'real-life' game, were two cars from my right, the father was tearing into some sort of pustules pock-marking his face. The children themselves had become impish demons still wearing the clothes of their human selves, but now with scarlet-red skin and yellow eyes, even having long thin tails wrapped around the safety bar.

Between us and the family, were the third-wheel and his lovebird friends. Third-wheel himself was pressed tightly against the left wall of his car screaming and trying to escape. His friends were now completely nude and pawing at each other while they kissed, as large leather wings filled most of the car's cabin space.

Just as I realized they had become a Succubus and Incubus, the car started to move once more, this time anti-clockwise, to which Cindy gave a groan of complaint because now I was 'winning', "Cindy! DID YOU SEE

Tilt-A-Whirl by M.B. Meraki

THE DEMONS!?"

"Demons? No! What are you talking about?" Cin looked at me like I was out of my mind, and perhaps it was because I couldn't believe the words that came out of my mouth next.

"The people on this ride are turning into demons! Imps! Succubus! Incubus! There was something wrong with the dad with the two kids, some sort of bumps on his face! But the kids were demons taunting him!"

Cindy frowned, "I thought we weren't going to do a 'real-life' on them, 'Leave the happy family alone,' you said."

"I'm not making up a story! I just saw them when we were switching directions. This is real!" I demanded though she shook her head and laughed at me.

"You need to stop watching horror movies," she scolded me and suddenly leaned hard against me to help make the car spin faster.

Could she be right? Was this all some flight of fancy in my mind? Maybe my cotton candy's paper tube had been laced with LSD? That *had* to be the case, there was no way people were becoming demons on a freaking Tilt-A-Whirl.

As we spun faster and faster the gravitational forces glued me to the metal wall of my car, and I could only watch the blurry world go by and listen to the screams I thought must really be in fun and laughter...

Until the blood splattered on me.

Fighting the spin was impossible at this rate. All I could do was gasp as the crimson fluid landed in a streak on my pale blue crop top and white shorts. I felt the wetness of it on my thigh.

I joined the chorus of screams and my panic grew when I looked at Cindy who was now blurry. Her skin had grown dark as if a shadow had fallen over her. Though the riot of lights should have burned away the shadows with each revolution of the car, she remained darker and she became translucent. Her once sky-blue eyes now shifted to an unholy glowing electric blue. Struggling to get away from her, I realized I barely felt the weight of her body against mine and as I tried to push her away, my hand went right through her.

That's when I felt the pain in my own bones, something was happening, shifting inside me, urgently trying to free itself from within me.

Looking down I saw my shirt was moving on its own, and below the crop top, my very skin was moving. Something was pushing around inside it, trying to get out like the chest-burster in *Alien*.

DEMONIC CARNIVAL

My screams were renewed with the excruciating pain of my flesh giving way to long, black spear-like protrusions clawing me open from the inside. Shooting pains in my leg-bones made me lurch forward to grab them. I was only vaguely aware that the ride was slowing down as my skin continued to be pierced by more protrusions at my stomach and lower gut. Every single part of me below my ribs felt like it was on fire.

The ride, at last, came to an end.

When the safety bar raised up, I grabbed tightly to it to try to pull myself out of the car, but I wound up pulling myself out of my own body.

White light burned behind my eyes, and my screams stopped momentarily as my breath was taken away. I felt as if the bones in my legs had been ripped out of my flesh...

Because they had.

I looked down and to my incredible horror saw the lower half of me; my waist, hips, groin, and legs with their torn and bloody shorts, were now hollow and slumped on the ground like a discarded pair of jeans. Immediately I retched up my supper, the splash landing on what I could see was now the front forelegs of a new body that had torn its way free of the former one. From the waist down I had become a spider, my torso attaching where the spider's head would have been, and my former body had been molted away like a spider's outgrown exoskeleton. I vaguely remembered the *Dungeons and Dragons Monster Manual* I read as a teen calling that combination a 'drider'. Eight legs twitched helplessly as I tried to figure out how to move them in a coordinated effort to stand up. I needed to stand up because standing up was the first step to running the hell out of this nightmare.

"Ooohh we have a celebrity among us tonight!" A stranger's voice interrupted my taking stock of my appalling new body. "The new incarnation of Fate is here! Everyone give a round of applause!"

I gazed rapidly around me, trying to figure out what was happening, still scrambling to try to get up on all eight of my new feet.

First thing I noticed, after the horrifying fact that I was a drider, was that to my right, third-wheel lay in a crumpled heap on the floor of the car he rode in. The Incubus and Succubus jointly feasting on what was left of his so recently beating heart.

Just beyond that grizzly scene, the father lay a groaning bloody mess at the feet of his imp children. The pustules on his face, I suddenly knew, without a doubt, were syphilis sores. He'd cheated on his wife and passed the disease on to her. How did I know that?

Snapping my head back to the left, poor Cindy floated over her own dead body, as she had become a ghost during this evil ride. She looked at her body with a sad sort of relief, "I took pills..." she suddenly confessed in a hollow voice, "I didn't think they'd kick in till after we got home. The ones I took yesterday only made me tired... so I took more tonight."

"What?! Why! Why would you kill yourself, Cin?!" I cried out and moved to grab her hands in mine. I missed, both because she was non-corporeal now and because I very much did not have control over the lower half of my body yet.

It was the juxtaposition of agony in my mind and body, and the wild cheering laughter and applause that made me look away from my best friend before she could give me the answer.

All of the Tilt-A-Whirl riders, even the ones I couldn't see during the brief pause in spinning, had become demons other than those already dead or dying. Beyond the ride stood other monsters; the tilt-man had ram's horns, the goth girl had dragon scales, the man in the suit had great black birdlike wings. The chaos in the Tilt-A-Whirl area seemed to be spreading throughout the entire carnival.

The panic in my mind finally picked out the fact that all the demons were all looking directly at me and cheering with excitement.

"It's you, Zoey," Cindy announced with unnerving certainty, "You are the new incarnation of Fate."

I didn't know how I knew, but I knew it was true. My silly imagination game of 'real-life' had come to haunt me, and I was now the weaver of Fate for all mankind. "Nnnnnnnooooo. Nope. No, thank you. This is just a nightmare and it's time to wake up now," I declared and looked around for things to change. I had been able to lucid dream my way out of nightmares since I had seen the movie *Dreamscape* as a child. Sure it terrified me, but it taught me you have to face your fears in your dreams and conquer them. So I turned to look at the demons around me, and summoned up all the courage I had, "This is not real, this is a dream, a horrible dream, and I banish you!" I screamed at the demons. Normally after I realized I was in a dream, I could change the terrifying aspects of the nightmare into harmless things; monsters into toys, darkness to light, blood to paint, but this time nothing was changing.

My eyes met the tilt-man's and he shook his head, "This is no dream. This is your new reality. You are, in fact, the incarnation of Fate," He said and gestured at the spider body. In folklore Fate was often represented by spiders because they 'weaved the threads of a person's life', but there were always three Fates; a child, an adult, and an old crone. Nowhere in the lore did anyone mention a half-spider person. "I don't believe you! You lie!" I fought back, and suddenly I became enormously tall because while my mind was distracted with my anger rather than being crippled by my fear, my body's natural instincts kicked in. Apparently along with the body came the knowledge of how to use it, so I was now standing seven feet tall. I pointed at him and with an open palm, I banished him as I did to my normal dream nightmares, "Back to whatever hell you came from!" I shouted and a pure white light flared up brightly to engulf him. Then when its brightness faded, there was no sign of the demonic tilt-man. "See! I knew it was a dream! Go BACK! All of you!" The demons each burned away in the powerful light. However, third-wheel's body still lay dead on the ground, the cheating father was still writhing in pain clutching his face, the dragon goth-girl and business suit man still stood where they were, and my poor Cindy was still a ghost hovering over her body.

That's when the man in the suit came closer, his black wings tucked neatly behind him, "You *are* Fate, you can force demons to return to their own dimensions, but this is real. Now you have to choose what you want to do with your newfound power."

"I don't want to be Fate! I want it to go back to the way it was!" I demanded as if it were still a dream I could control.

The winged man sighed softly, "You can't go back, but you can undo everything else that has happened here when the clock struck midnight. Your friend, the boy with a broken heart, the cheating father, dragon-girl, and all the others throughout the carnival who were affected by the curse can go back to the way they were. You can undo it all and rework the tapestry of their lives so that they have a better outcome."

"Are you really the incarnation of Pride like I thought?" My voice had weakened, suddenly sounding smaller, much more timid and my body was lowering itself to the ground as my anger turned to fear causing me to shrink back in a defensive manner.

Laughter peppered the air, but it wasn't a laugh of merriment at all, it was sad laughter, "I am not, that's why I wasn't banished. I am Death, I am here to escort the souls to their final destinations. Unless of course, you choose to undo their deaths."

"Fate can't do that, once a thread has been cut, that's it," I stated.

"That's what modern media would have you believe, but it isn't the truth. So what will it be? Will it be *me* who gets to work, or *you*?"

Looking at my friend then the other victims of what was apparently a curse that took hold at midnight, and back to the man who said he was Death incarnate. This was all insane, too insane, but maybe it was real?

Somehow—deep in my soul—I knew it was real. Just like I knew the father had cheated on his wife, that the goth girl was a dragon shifter because she wished to 'not be powerless anymore', and that Cindy had killed herself because she'd been sexually abused by her step-brother and felt death was the only escape. "Cin, why didn't you tell me what was happening to you?"

Cindy shook her head and looked down at her body, "He said if I told, he would say I was a whore and slept around, blaming these fake guys for whatever he did to me."

That did it. That made my choice for me and I brought myself up to my full new seven-foot tall height. I looked at Death and said with determination, "I've got a lot of work to do, show me how to do it."

ABOUT THE AUTHOR

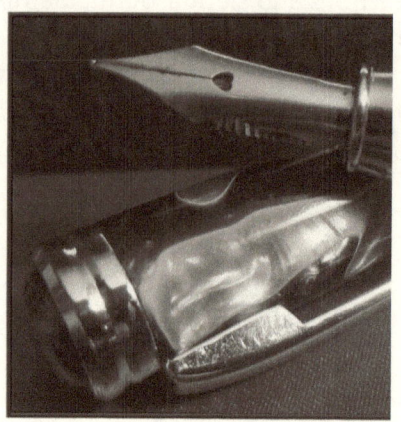

.B. Meraki had been toiling away as a technical writer and artist for various magazines, and advertising companies for nearly two decades, all the while creating artwork and various creative writing for private clients.

After joining a very supportive writer's group, M.B. began to share the more creative works and after getting positive feedback and winning some local contests, decided to pursue the dream of becoming a full-time time writer. Slowly M.B. is converting the hundreds of short stories hidden away in stacks of spiral notebooks into full fantasy fiction stories to share with others.

Publication in this anthology is an honor, and if you're interested in contacting the author, please send an email to mbmeraki@gmail.com

THE MIRROR MAZE

Stephen Herczeg

"Come on Debbie, I wanna go to the Tunnel of Love," Billy said, his voice slurring due to the half quart of scotch he'd drunk before they'd entered the fairground. Debbie smiled, her eyes a little bleary from her own share of the scotch.

"We can go to the Tunnel of Love later, lover boy," she said, "I know exactly why you want to go in there, but you can just wait."

She poked him in the chest after concentrating for a few seconds so she could focus and make proper contact. Billy simply anchored his sight and balance on the tight sweater that Debbie wore. He smiled at the thought of the Tunnel of Love and nodded.

"Okay, we'll do what you want first," he said, his mind happy to agree with anything for the time being as long as they ended up where his intentions lay.

They walked across the open field surrounded by the temporary fairground's attractions. Debbie made a beeline for the Mirror Maze. They stopped outside and peered at the curved mirrors on display. Side by side they were reflected in different shaped mirrors.

Debbie's normally short and buxom frame was stretched into a bean pole by the mirror before her. She towered over Billy's reflection which had turned his normally tall and athletic frame into a squat, flattened blob of a boy.

Debbie burst out laughing and snorted at the images before them.

"You look fat. I bet you've never looked fat before."

Billy looked more offended than amused. Debbie saw his serious expression and laughed even more. Another snort produced a small gout of snot from her nose.

Billy saw it and feigned being grossed out while holding back a roaring laugh.

"Not funny," Debbie said embarrassed while she fished around in her handbag for a tissue. She recovered quickly and smiled a big cheesy grin at Billy.

"I wanna go in here," she said indicating the Mirror Maze.

Billy grimaced.

"Really?" he said.

Debbie stood with her hands on her hips, an insistent look on her face. Billy stared at the set features of her face, his eyes slipping lower momentarily. He noticed that the rest of her had as much of an indignant posture as her face. He felt a stirring deep inside and remembered the reward on offer if he placated Debbie's every whim.

He looked back into her eyes and smiled. He made sure he effected his lopsided grin, the one that broke every girl's heart.

"Okay."

Debbie's stern gaze softened.

They turned and moved up to the ticket booth. A grizzled old man, with long hanks of greasy hair hanging down from his balding scalp, greeted them.

"How can I help yous?" he said.

"Two tickets to the Maze, please," Debbie said as Billy fished out some money.

"Ah, you'll love it in the Maze," the Old Man said, "You could be lost in there for hours, days maybe, but don't worry yeselves though, we'll send in the police after a week or so."

Billy stopped.

"You're not serious are you?" he asked concern on his face.

Debbie thumped him playfully on the arm.

"He's just joking silly," she said.

Billy looked at the man.

"Are you?" he asked, suddenly unsure about entering the maze.

"Not scared are ye sonny? A smart looking boy like ye should have no trouble finding ye way outta there," he said, a sly grin on his lips.

The Mirror Maze by Stephen Herczeg

Billy puffed out his chest and stretched himself to full height trying to both impress the old man and hide any fear he felt. The old man chuckled, a thick raspy chuckle full of mucous.

"Don't worry son, you'll be fine, but I guarantee ye won't come out the same person as ye goes in," he said with another chuckle.

Debbie giggled to herself and said, "That'll work won't it, Billy? Change is good. I could always use a new man."

Billy looked at her for a moment. He felt put upon on both sides and was feeling less happy with entering the Maze. Debbie noticed. Her playful nature came to the fore and she whispered a reminder into Billy's ear, intentionally pressing herself against his arm.

"How much?" Billy snapped, suddenly much happier to get in and out of the maze.

"Five bucks for the two o' ya," the old man said.

Billy slapped down the money and the two entered.

"Enjoy yourselves. Don't be fooled by the mirrors, they only reflect what they see. And they see all," the old man called out.

Debbie hugged Billy's arm as she led him through the entrance. Billy stared back at the old man for a moment, trying to work out what he'd meant by his last statement.

Another tug on his arm and he entered the maze.

The first area was a large circular room lined with long rectangular mirrors. Each mirror was curved so that the couple's reflections changed from long and tall to short and squat.

Debbie stopped by each mirror and laughed at the way her body changed shape in each one.

"Would you like me if I was fat," she asked in front of a mirror that made her look nine months pregnant.

Billy saw the image, horror came to his face. Debbie saw it and laughed.

"Well you better be careful with little Billy, then," she said.

She grabbed his arm and dragged him before each of the mirrors in turn, laughing as he changed shape and at times merged into her reflection.

Billy turned his head slightly, then snapped it around. He was sure he'd seen movement out of the corner of his eye. Something strange had appeared in a mirror on the other side of the room. His head spun a little from all the weird reflections and the alcohol.

He broke away from Debbie and staggered a little towards the mirror. He stared deep into it, his own reflection appearing upside down. He wasn't sure what he saw, but it seemed small and a strange shade of green. An alien object amongst the gaudy yellow paint, shiny surfaces and dirt floor.

Debbie laughed at herself, then noticed Billy.

"What's wrong?" she called over her shoulder.

"I don't think we're alone in here," he said.

"Well there's lots of people in the Fairground, so not really that shocking," she said as she moved to another mirror and burst out laughing.

Billy moved from mirror to mirror looking in the reflections and peering into the cracks between them. He noticed that there was nobody behind him and turned.

Debbie was gone.

He hurried across the room and searched for any corridors leading away. He finally found two mirrors that hid a gap behind them and ducked into the passageway. As expected it was lined with more mirrors and the odd pane of plain glass that allowed the customer to peer into an adjacent room or corridor.

He searched all along the hallway, stopping to peer through into any rooms as he went, but there was no sign of Debbie anywhere.

He yelled, "Debbie?"

A distant voice greeted him, yelling his name back.

"Stay where you are. I'll come to you," he said.

"No, this is fun, you have to find me, that's if you want me, lover boy," was the reply.

Billy's face distorted in anger at the reply. He charged down the corridor, turning several times before finding himself in another circular room. This one was lined with plain mirrors that reflected his image in every pane of glass.

He turned and faced his multiple doppelgangers.

There must be another corridor out.

He moved up to the nearest mirror and touched it. He stepped to one side and tried every mirror until he'd completed a full circuit of the room.

He realised that he hadn't found the way he'd come in.

What the hell?

He tried every pane of glass again. Each was solid with no gaps between it and its neighbour. He pushed at each one in turn, thinking they must swing away to reveal the exit.

Nothing. Every one of them was as solid as its neighbour.

The Mirror Maze by Stephen Herczeg

What is going on?

"Debbie?" he yelled out.

No answer.

He turned and looked around the myriad reflections of himself. Each one seemed to stare back at him with glints of ridicule in their eyes, not the despondent and fearful stare Billy knew was on his face.

He ran up to the nearest mirror and pressed his hand against it. The reflection failed to mirror his action, instead staying well back and sneering at him.

Billy reeled back in horror.

The reflection stepped back, pointed and laughed a silent laugh at him.

Anger boiled over the terror building in Billy's mind. He launched forward and slammed his fist into the mirror, shattering the laughing reflection into a thousand pieces.

He dragged his hand back through the frame. A shard of glass nicked his flesh and blood sprayed from the deep cut.

Billy cried in pain and cradled his hand to his chest. He looked down at the seeping wound then up at the shattered mirror.

The glass was whole again.

His reflection stood before him, holding its own hand to its chest and mimicking Billy's expression of shock and pain.

Confused, Billy realised it must have all been a dream. He held out his hand. Blood spilled from the wound and dripped to the dry, dirt floor.

He looked up at his reflection.

It stared back at him, its hand outstretched with blood dripping down to the same dirt floor. A sad pained look on its face, that suddenly split into a wide grin. Billy's reflection moved the hand up to its mouth. A long-pointed tongue snaked out and ran along the wound, lapping at the blood and disappearing back into the mouth.

This isn't happening. It's not real.

Pained and scared, Billy stepped closer to the smiling reflection. He reached out with his good hand and touched the glass. It was solid.

It's in my mind. The scotch. I just drank too much.

His head swam. He closed his eyes to let it clear. When he opened them again he saw Debbie's reflection walking behind his own in the mirror. He turned and stared across the room. There she was. In the mirror opposite.

It must be pane of glass. She's in the next room.

"Debbie," he yelled.

DEMONIC CARNIVAL

The image turned towards him. Debbie's face lit up as she saw Billy. She waved at him and beckoned.

"Debbie I'm coming," he said and ran towards her. His feet tangled themselves up and pitched him forward. He saw the mirror frame grow in his vision and braced himself for impact. He landed with a bone-crunching thud on the dirt floor and slowly picked himself up.

He looked around. No Debbie.

Then he spied the mirror frame. His reflection stood staring back at him again. It leered at him with a mouthful of wickedly pointed teeth and held out a completely healed arm. It waved at Billy and walked out through a newly opened passageway.

Billy rushed up to the mirror and thumped helplessly against the glass surface.

He spun and stared all around. He realised he was inside the mirror. He ran to each corner of the reflected room. There was no exit. No escape. Only more mirrors. He banged on each in turn, hoping to break them. In this reflected world he had no power and no hope.

Billy's reflection stepped out through the entrance and found Debbie standing near the ticket booth. Her face brightened when she saw him, and she hurried over grabbing him around the waist.

"I thought you'd never get out of there, what happened?" she asked.

Billy shrugged.

The old man turned to Debbie and said, "I told you he'd get out of there eventually. He's a real keeper this one. Sharp as a tack, I reckons."

Debbie looked at the old man, then at Billy. She loved him dearly, but the old man was right.

"Anyways, well done there young man," said the old man.

He held up a ticket and offered it to Billy.

"For surviving the Mirror Maze, you can have a free ticket to the Tunnel of Love. Just tell them Jethro sent ya and give 'em that," he said.

Billy took it and smiled. Debbie took his arm and wrapped it around her shoulder and began to lead him away.

"Come on, let's get to the Tunnel of Love before they close it. It's getting cold and I need you to keep me warm," she said.

The old man in the ticket booth, coughed once. Billy looked over his shoulder at him. He smiled showing his needle-like teeth. His long tongue snaked out of his mouth and flicked at the air before retracting. He free hand thrust out to the side and transformed into a scaled hand with five long taloned fingers which he flicked open and closed before it morphed back into a human hand.

"You two have fun now. It's a long tunnel, but not too long," he said with a wink at Billy and a chuckle to himself.

Billy turned back and pulled Debbie closer to him as they headed towards the Tunnel of Love.

The old man glanced at the mirrors lining the outside of the Maze. Dozens of young men, all about Billy's age, appeared across the entire wall. They wailed silently at the old man. Several rushed forwards and slammed into the mirrors with no effect.

"Now, there's no need to get yeselves upset, I tells ye. You've only got yeselves to blame for getting lost. Smart peoples gets out of the maze, so why couldn't yous," he said as a tall blonde boy slammed into the mirror with his shoulder and rocked back half stunned.

Billy stepped into view.

The old man moved up to the wall.

"Hey there young fella, welcome to the Mirror Maze. I told ye you'd come out a different person," he said with a raucous laugh.

Billy screamed silently.

The End

ABOUT THE AUTHOR

Stephen is an IT Geek, writer, actor, film maker and Taekwondo Black Belt based in Canberra Australia. He has been writing for over twenty years and has completed a couple of dodgy novels, sixteen feature length screenplays and dozens of short stories and scripts.

Stephen's scripts, *TITAN, Dark are the Woods, Control* and *Death Spores* have found success in international screenwriting competitions with a win, two runner-up and two top ten finishes.

His horror stories have featured in various anthologies including: *Sproutlings; Hells Bells; Trickster's Treats #1* and *#2; Shades of Santa;*

Below the Stairs; Behind the Mask; Beyond the Infinite; Beside the Seaside; The Body Horror Book; Anemone Enemy; Petrified Punks; Beginnings; and *Sea of Secrets*.

Over thirty of his drabbles have been accepted for *Curses and Cauldrons* by *Blood Song Books*; and *Worlds; Angels; Monsters; Beyond* & *Unravel* by *Black Hare Press*.

His Sherlock Holmes stories have been published in *Sherlock Holmes in the realms of H.G. Wells, Sherlock Holmes: Adventures beyond the Canon, The MX Book of New Sherlock Holmes stories: Part XI; Sherlock Holmes: Adventures in the realms of Steampunk, The MX Book of New Sherlock Holmes stories: Part XIV* and *The New Adventures of Solar Pons*.

Later this year, Stephen will appear in the anthologies *A Tribute to H.G. Wells; Journeys; Capricorn; Aquarius; Deep Space* and *Through Death's Door*.

Stephen's Amazon author page can be found here: https://www.amazon.com/-/e/B07916SQQS

You can catch Stephen at his Facebook page: https://www.facebook.com/stephenherczegauthor

THE DEVIL'S DUE

Kerilyn Blake

The ride looked out of place among the cheery lights of 'Ride Alley', a weather-beaten banner announcing the name of the long line of rides before them. The ride was at the end of the corridor out of the way of all the "fun" rides. Placed between the Fun House and the Haunted Mansion it looked as if they were trying to hide the dilapidated ride away from the rainbows of happy flashing lights, whirring sound effects and loud music. He felt sorry for the poor thing, with its outdated look and horrified screams piped out of somewhere to make it seem interesting. The ride operator looked bored, sitting on an old barstool, smoking a cigarette.

"It's so cute," Frankie said beside him.

"It looks like a death trap," Joel replied.

"Oh come on! There's hardly a line, and you know I love the cheesy rides!"

"What does it even do, Frankie?"

Joel sighed as he looked at the ride again, and at the four others milling around the ride, seeming to wait for a few more people to show interest in the ride before they committed to stand in line.

"I don't know. Let's find out. Come on! Please?"

"Fine," He muttered in surrender and followed Frankie toward the entrance to the ride. He knew that if Frankie had her heart set on something changing her mind was like brushing your teeth while eating Oreos—simply impossible. Pulling off a ticket for each of them from the strip of tickets in his hand, he offered it to the grubby man, "What does this ride do?" He asked.

"It goes around and around. You try not to slip off the wheel while it's spinning. If you do, you hit the wall. Last one on the top of the wheel wins." The operator responded in a monotone voice as he took the tickets, depositing them into a garbage can beside the stool.

"Joy," Joel said with an eye roll and stepped inside with Frankie.

The ride was illuminated by a few electric candles mounted on the dark walls that looked as if they came with the ride when it was built seventy some years ago. They cast off just enough light in the room to see the raised circular pattern on the floor. Two small speakers in opposite corners of the room were held onto a rickety looking iron cage with bent clothes hangers, playing recordings of frightened screams on a loop.

A nudge from Frankie had him stepping down onto the platform. "C'mon! It's going to be fun!" Frankie urged as the couple extra people ventured through the doors and joined them on the platform. The metal doors closed with a slam, taking the light with it and making Frankie jump in surprise at the loud noise. He snickered at her as they sat down on the wheel, earning him a punch in the arm.

"I'm going to win this ride," he leaned in to whisper to Frankie.

"No, you're not," she whispered back, her voice a quiet challenge.

The electric candles started to flicker as the ride groaned to life with a jerk. He held onto the spinning platform with a steady grip as the speed increased. He felt Frankie try to grip his arm and hold on, but it was no use. Frankie and the other people on the ride slipped off the wheel a few seconds later.

"Ha!" He called out to Frankie. "I won! Just like I said I would!" He called out triumphantly to her.

He found it harder to keep his grip on the smooth wheel, not only because vertigo started to impair his equilibrium but because his palms were starting to sweat with the heat that the floor was starting to radiate under him.

He knew that something was going wrong when the smell of the smoke and the sound of the metal grinding on metal filled the room.

Great, he thought as he felt the wheel under them start to wobble, *we're going to burn alive in a ride that hasn't been serviced since the 1900's.*

"Frankie! Go get some help!" He called out as he held on but heard no reply.

Sparks illuminated the room and acrid smoke hovered in the air. A few seconds later, the ride ground to a painful halt, and took what little light was left in the room with it.

"Oh, this was a *GREAT* ride Fr-"

The wheel went off kilter and listed to the side and had him digging his fingernails into the once the smooth surface of the wheel. Horrible sounds of wood cracking and metal groaning as it bent under the wheel made his heart skip a beat as he tried to slide himself off the wheel and onto the safety of the platform.

CRACK!

A gasp escaped his lips as the sudden feeling of freefall as his foot missed the platform made an awful sinking feeling in his stomach. "Frankie!!" He screamed as he lost grip of the wheel. His fear-filled screams were stolen from him by a wind that whipped his hair backward against his ears and cheeks as he fell. The smoke in the air became heavier and he gasped to take a breath, a sulfur taste suffocating him as he tried to pull air into his lungs. His vision blurred and his consciousness faded...

He woke up to the feeling of a cold, hard floor underneath him. A naked lightbulb above him offered enough light to see his surroundings. He sat up and looked around the room. A single table and chair in the middle, bare walls and a single door on the far wall.

Holy shit. He was alive. But... how did he survive the fall?

Where the hell was he?

Hearing approaching footsteps, he got to his feet. The sound of a lock popping free drew his attention to the door across the room. A tall, emaciated man dressed in a black pinstriped business suit entered the room through the open door. Joel opened his mouth to speak, but the man simply held up a bony hand to silence Joel and cleared his throat "Save any questions you have, as all will be answered when it is your turn." His voice was a frail, wispy tone that made Joel strain to hear what he was saying.

"Please, follow me."

Joel frowned but followed the man out the door, taking in his surroundings as he walked down a long corridor. *Where the hell did I end up?* Joel thought to himself. He saw nothing that stuck out to tell him where he was. Eggshell colored walls were devoid of everything leading to many closed doors, accented with mahogany trims and floorboards. The smell of old books, furniture polish and the eerie silence reminded him of a library or courtroom.

Joel's question was answered when they reached a large wooden door that stood open before them. On the other side of the door was a court-room. He saw a judge seated behind a bench dressed in a powdered wig and black flowing robes. The bench seemed to stretch upwards so high that Joel had to crane his neck upwards to see the judge. Two long tables in front of the bench, one of them occupied by a clown, a serious clown face painted perfectly, a polka-dotted business suit and jester's shoes completed the outfit. Behind the tables were a jury bench filled with a mixture of men and women, faces absolutely void of emotion.

Joel laughed out loud as he felt the whole situation was ridiculous. Lawyers dressed up as a clown and a skeleton. Standing in a courtroom in… wherever he was, he had no idea where he was. His laughter faded quickly as the clown turned to look at him as he laughed and flashed him a set of blood red stained row of razor-sharp shark's teeth behind the face painted lips.

Joel was led behind the empty table, his lawyer taking his place beside him. The sound of a gavel from above them cracked through the air and demanded the attention of all in the courtroom. The effect was imme-diate, a shiver of absolute silence spread across the room. Not a cough, not a breath could be heard.

"Joel Powers," the voice of the judge echoed through the room, cold and accusing. "You are charged with one count of murder."

He felt his eyebrows pop up so high, he swore he lost them in his hair-line. "I'm sorry, what? Murder!?" He stammered, his gaze turning to his lawyer beside him. "I haven't murdered anyone! I got on a ride called the 'Devil's Due' with Frankie. It broke down and I fell through the floor and ended up here! I am innocent of what I'm being accused of. I'm standing behind a table, being accused of murder while being stared down by a terrifying clown with teeth that would shred a large man apart, and *I'm* the one accused of killing someone?" He felt his stomach do another flip as he looked away from him and faced the judge once more.

What the HELL was going on here!

The feeling of his heart pounding in his chest grew as he watched his pinstriped lawyer calmly pull a file out of his briefcase and slowly set it on the table. He faced the judge as he seemed to ignore Joel's comment completely.

"Your Honor, my client wishes to plead innocent."

"You're damned right I'm innocent!" Joel shouted out at the judge, leaning his hands against the table. "I don't even know who I'm supposed to have killed."

The Prosecutor spoke with surprising eloquence behind those razor-sharp teeth, "Your Honor, the victim, Frankie…"

"Frankie? I didn't kill Frankie!" Joel interrupted.

"…Joseph's strangled body was found by her neighbor at her place of residence, 165 Brightmanshire Road."

Joel's eyes widened as he stared at the clown lawyer in stunned silence for a moment before he turned his eyes up to the Judge. "Your honor, I did not murder Frankie. The last time I saw her, we were getting on a ride at a carnival called Devil's Due, just a few minutes ago! I couldn't have killed her. I swear to God, she was alive and well the last time I saw her!"

There was another silent pause before Joel's lawyer cleared his throat. "Your honor, I would like to request a recess so that my client may make use of our research facilities and review the evidence in this case, and to find evidence to support his pleas of innocence."

The judge's attention turned to the prosecutor, who replied, "We would support this recess, your honor."

"Granted." The voice above boomed out, and the sound of the gavel echoed around the room once more. Everyone but Joel and his lawyer stood and filed out of the courtroom. As the lawyer picked up the file, a side door opened, and a wedge of bright light pierced through the darkness of the courtroom.

"What's going on? What's that for? What do I have to prove? Isn't it innocent until proven guilty?" Joel fired off question after question as he looked at his lawyer.

"Not here." The attorney said as he turned to look at Joel. "You have already been found guilty of the crime. Now, it is up to you to prove otherwise. Those are the rules here. The research library will answer any questions you have and give you any evidence that you may need to try and prove your innocence."

"Where is here?" Joel asked

"Here is where you prove that you didn't murder your friend," He said and motioned at the wedge of light, "You're wasting time."

Joel moved out from behind the table and walked to the door. Pushing it open fully, he squinted at the nearly blinding light. Blinking a few times to help adjust his vision to the bright light, he heard a female voice beside him.

"Welcome."

The Devil's Due by Kerilyn Blake

Jumping in surprise, he turned his head to the source of the voice and was met with a pair of haunting green eyes behind a pale face. Glancing down at her, he noticed the emaciated woman dressed in a simple white dress that hung off her body. Her thin grey hair was pulled up in a tight bun. A small smile of apology touched her blue-tinted lips.

"I am Lilly. I will be your guide here to help you with your search. If you would be so kind as to follow me," she said, leading Joel away from the door.

Looking around the room as she led him to an empty desk in the first row of endless tables that seemed to go on as far as the eye could see. Many people sat in chairs at different tables in the room, all of them in various states of distress. The man across from his table seemed to be hard at work, staring down at a book with red-rimmed bloodshot eyes as he scribbled notes on a note pad. A woman scrubbed her hands through her hair as she stared down at the book as thick as *War and Peace*. Another chewed their nails as they flipped through a book with their other hand. All of them looked to be searching for something that they were having trouble finding. He noted that everyone sitting at a table had someone like Lilly standing beside their desk.

Joel looked back at her with a frown, "Where am I?" He asked her as he sat down in the chair.

"You are in the hall of records," Lilly said simply, her hands clasped neatly in front of her.

"I see. Can you tell me why am I here?"

"You are here to find proof that you are innocent of the crime that you have been convicted of,"

"Aren't you innocent until proven guilty?"

"Not here," she said quietly. "Your soul bears the weight of the sin. Now, it is up to you to prove that it was not your sin. Though, most who do look for proof find more than they were looking for."

"But... I haven't done anything wrong! I just got on this stupid ride and ended up here."

"Well, we could check the case records," Lilly suggested with an encouraging smile and left Joel at the table, returning a short time later carrying with her a vintage 1970's Sony Solid State Portable TV. She set it on the table, turned the device toward Joel who watched the little screen come to life. Leaning in, he watched as the video started to play on the black and white screen.

DEMONIC CARNIVAL

The image faded in with Joel standing on Frankie's porch, knocking on the door. Not hearing an answer, he knocked again, a little louder in case she didn't hear him the first time. Each time he knocked; he grew a little more irritated. He hated being ignored.

Opening the door with a look of nervous surprise on her face, Frankie asked, "What are you doing here, Joel?" Holding a pink silk robe closed with her left hand, she held the door open just wide enough to stand between the door and the frame.

She seemed to be hiding something.

"We had a date," he said as he stood in front of the door, rocking to the side slightly and trying to sneak a peek inside her house.

"I told you I'm not feeling well," Frankie explained as she rested her hip against the door, noticing his actions and denying him the glance into her house.

"Someone's here," Joel said suspiciously.

"No Joel, there isn't anyone here," Frankie repeated. "I'll call you tomorrow. Okay? We can talk about it then."

Anger set in and he frowned, "We can talk about this now."

Joel pushed Frankie into the house, hearing the door bounce against the wall roughly. The lights on the foyer's wall exploded as the heavy door hit the wall. Screams of fright filled his ears as Frankie fell backward on the hardwood floor. He stomped into the house after her, leaving the door open, grabbed the lapels of her robe and lifted her up. Looking down, he could see a white satin nightdress under the pink silk robe he held open in his hands.

"Where is he, Frankie?" He shouted, crushing the gentle fabric in his fists and giving her a shake, "Women don't wear satin unless there's a reason!"

Fighting to get away from his grasp she pushed against him, "There's nobody here, I swear to you." She said in a nervous, shaky voice. "But... Since you're already here, why don't you stay here tonight? It'll be just you and me?" She offered, her hands trembling as she touched his shoulder while he stared at her intently, holding her so roughly, "Come on, Joel! It's going to be fun."

The rage calmed inside of him at her offer, and he let go of the silk slowly. "Just you and me? Alone?"

Nodding her head quickly, moist blue eyes stared at him with fear. "Alone." She agreed.

Standing her up properly and setting her back up on her feet, he smoothed out the fragile fabric that had been crumpled in his fists. "I'm sorry. I just lost my head," reaching up to catch the tear that slipped from her eye with his thumb. "You really are beautiful in this—"

The shadow of something in his peripheral vision caused his head to snap to the side and try to catch whatever it was that he saw. Looking into the living room he saw the light from the group of candles flickering beside a book that sat on the coffee table. A gentle breeze blew through an open window, waving a thin lace curtain inward.

"YOU LIED!" He bellowed and glared at Frankie, "There is someone here!" He grabbed her wrist and hauled her forward, shoving Frankie into the room.

Stumbling into the room, Frankie flailed to catch herself, landing on and breaking the glass coffee table. With the glass and the items from atop the table stabbing into her back, she screamed as he straddled her "Joel! Please!" she begged, "There's nobody here. I opened the window."

"Liar! They escaped out the window. "

Frankie struggled under him, the corners of the book pressing into her lower back painfully. She could only pray that the pregnancy test was still hidden under it.

"Stop lying to me!" he said, putting his hands around her throat, pressing down tightly. "Admit that you have someone here!"

Frankie coughed as his hands started to block her from breathing, her throat collapsing as he squeezed tighter. Fingernails scratched at his hands in a futile attempt to get free.

"Tell me what I want to know!" He yelled down at her, spittle flying as he lost control.

Joel looked away from the screen. "That… That didn't happen. We came to the carnival. We ate cotton candy and went on these cheesy stupid rides."

"Do you remember how you got here, Joel?" Lilly asked.

Joel frowned as he looked down at the table, scrubbing his hands through his hair. "We walked down the long road of rides."

"Not to the ride, Joel. How did you get to the Carnival?"

Joel blinked at the tabletop as he tried to remember, scrubbed his hands through his hair. "I don't remember, Lilly. I don't remember anything."

"You don't remember, because Frankie's neighbor killed you to try and save her. What you didn't see while you had your hands around her throat was that she was pregnant with your child. That's why she was not feeling well, and why she was so apprehensive to open the door. She was afraid to tell you the truth; you died taking Frankie's life. Both of your souls ended up here, in purgatory. You both took a ride on the Devil's Wheel. She spun off of the wheel. Her soul is free. Your soul stayed with us, weighed down by sin."

Joel shook his head in denial.

"You now have proof explaining why you were here, but the outcome wasn't what you expected. The Devil wants his due, Joel. Your soul will be a great addition to the Dark Carnival."

"Welcome home."

ABOUT THE AUTHOR

Kerilyn Blake is a small town girl from Saskatchewan, Canada, with a passion for the written word. Always found with her nose in a book in her youth, her passion for writing started when she was introduced to D&D as a teenager and then eventually to role play by her now husband. The ability to stretch the imagination freely with a group of people who enjoyed like interests stirred an interest in creating stories in the fantasy and science fiction world.

When she is not baking, cooking or keeping order within the chaos of keeping a house filled with 3 children and 2 fur babies, Kerilyn enjoys spending time role playing with her best friend or reading novels from the horror, thriller or paranormal romance genre from favorite authors like Stephen King, Dean Koontz, J.R. Ward, and Lara Adrian. If you would like to contact the author, you may send Kerilyn an email at kerilynblake@gmail.com.

THE ARCHITECT SCORNED

Larry Griffin

The carnival was new in Silver Lake, Montana, and everyone had been slowing down in their cars, craning their necks to see the spectacle. All those big gleaming hulks, dragged out into the sunlight. Shining reds and blues and greens, the rides and the tents, and soon the entire lot of the fairgrounds, half a mile east of the Interstate, was covered. It would be a new day for Silver Lake, one with actual fun and camaraderie, not just the lazy, docile farmer's market of old.

The problem was that they did not have anyone to inspect the rides, to make sure things were going smooth. Montana, it turned out, had no agency for that sort of thing. It was like the Wild West in that way. They ended up asking a local architect, Myron Spoons, who was known for helping to renovate several of the town's historic buildings in the last several years. They'd pay him a small salary, it was decided at the town council meeting, and he would make sure everything was hunky dory.

Myron was an introvert, whose parents had long since departed for Florida, to bask in the sun in their golden years. But he liked the rustic character of Silver Lake. He'd wanted to become an architect from a young age because he had just always enjoyed how things were built; houses or cars or whatever. He would spend his elementary school days marveling at the construction of the school, of its smooth walls, detailed slats and high-arched windows. What must it have been like to build *that*, way back in the day? The logic and thought that went into each wall, each brick, each architectural decision, fascinated him endlessly.

But he'd never been good with people. They made no sense to him. All of them, just odd bags of meat and flesh and he did not know how to connect with them. His teachers in school would find him climbed up onto the smaller roof area, hand caressing the slats and the outer rim, and would shout, "Myron, get down from there!" and he would be snapped out of his trance, yanked painfully into the harsh and cold reality.

So Myron walked the fairgrounds and chatted with the newly-hired carnival workers. They were mostly sketchy drifters, guys with priors who had wanted a job where they wouldn't have to disclose them. Or guys who wanted to eat cheap and needed a place to stay, and Silver Lake did have an abundance of affordable housing.

But Myron mostly cared about the rides. He looked up at the Fireball with its giant metallic claw of passenger seats, and the red hue of the exterior, and thought *it's the most beautiful thing I've ever seen.*

Across town at that moment, a young woman named Rose Edmonds was moving into her family's ancestral home. Her grandmother had just passed away that previous week, and in her will, had given Rose the house; a great behemoth of the Victorian era, all dark wood and towers on the top and big windows. It looked to her like a castle, and it was situated out in the country, sitting on two dozen acres of land, all rolling plains that a pre-paid team would tend to, they'd assured her.

But she did not know what to do with the house at all. She was used to small apartments, cramped with roommates to fight the high rents of the city. It was summer now, though, and she wanted a different experience, a change of pace. She had been writing a novel, anyway. Maybe a change in scenery would be good.

She walked the old house, checking out the dusty, expansive rooms with their archaic carpeting over hard wood, the love-seats that dated back to when her parents were children, the lacy curtains with floral patterns that let plenty of light in.

And it was all so... *overwhelming.*

She needed something familiar.

And so she plopped down on the couch in the living room, ignoring the dust that shot up like a volcanic geyser, and pulled out her phone. And she began to swipe on Tinder. The selection in Silver Lake was, unsurprisingly, not extensive.

Myron didn't even know what the little flame icon on his cell phone meant when he pulled it out to check the time. It was only after a few moments that he remembered he'd installed Tinder on a lark, while drunk one night a while back. This was the first match he'd ever gotten. Her name was Rose, and she was pretty with dark hair and dark eyes.

He was still standing at the carnival. Something was telling him to go ahead and message her, take a chance. He looked up at the Fireball. *Was that you?* He asked.

No answer – not in words, anyway. But he was filled with a knowledge that the Fireball had been the thing speaking to him.

Okay, he thought. I'll give it a shot. But only because *you* told me to.

Rose and Myron agreed to meet up at an Italian diner, one of the newer restaurants in Silver Lake, opened up by a chef who had just really harbored a fantasy about living in a rural nowhere-town and had made his dreams come true. Myron found that inspiring, and enjoyed the fact that he didn't have to drive three hours for it, like he did with other types of cuisine enjoyed.

Rose was shy at first, and she found Myron to be nicely unpretentious – he didn't try, like a lot of guys, to come off ultra-masculine or to impress her in some ridiculous way. They just talked over breadsticks and white wine. She told him about her book: "It's a coming of age story about a girl finding out who she really is. And then she learns that the town is under siege by vampires, so she has to learn kung fu to kill them all."

"Fascinating," Myron said.

On a courageous spur of the moment decision, Rose invited him to come back to the house. She figured why not, she didn't know anyone here, might as well explore some different parts of herself. And if nothing happened, well, then it would be but an odd story, an anecdote to tell of later.

And so they went back to the old Victorian. And that was when Myron fell in love.

He had never seen anything like it. The dark majesty of it, and the sheer *grace*.

If anything, it woke him up. Inside, on the couch, they began to feel each other up and have some fun. And then they were going up to her room, entangled legs and arms on the stairs, a spider-like creature making its way through the old tomb of the house.

Undressed and on the bed, they made love. And with every thrust Myron was looking not at Rose, but up at the walls and the foundation of the room. God, he thought; what a marvel the house was.

They continued to date for a week after that. The carnival was not yet open, but residents were salivating for it. They would line up at the gates and stare and marvel, and some of them would remark that they felt such an odd *compulsion* when they were near the carnival rides, like they were out of their own bodies, but they shook it off and went back to the pub or their homes to watch re-runs of M.A.S.H. and Agatha Christie like any other day. The carnival would come in time. They were not impatient, they reminded themselves.

Myron and Rose were at the movie theater, catching the latest super-hero movie which they forgot about the moment they exited the theater, and Myron asked if she wanted to go back to her place again.

"I dunno," she said. "I've just been spending so much time there. Can we go to yours?"

He shrugged and became sullen. That did not excite him as much. She figured they would talk about it after the movie, but after that they both decided they were tired, and went their separate ways.

She figured he just didn't want her to see his messy cluttered room. But then the whole thing began to unravel. Myron became distant and Rose had to roll her eyes; she'd seen it so many times before. He was out for the shallow thing, the experience of sex like a conquest.

And they hadn't seen each other for about a week when a college friend of hers told her about a guy she knew, a friend, who seemed like Rose's type. Rose shrugged and made the trek back to big Butte, Montana, where she'd gone to school, and met her old friend and her friend's boyfriend and the new guy, Ryan, a transplant from Oklahoma who'd come to work on his doctorate. Ryan was handsome and funny and a bit reserved, the right kind of reserved, and Rose found herself wanting to see him again.

So they began to trade off, seeing each other on weekends. She would drive to him one week and he to her the next. In between, it was a lot of texts, a lot of WhatsApp and Skype.

Myron continued inspecting the fair, focusing all his energy on that. It was here that he began to see the spirits more clearly.

He supposed they had always been there, whispering to him as he walked among the set-up tents for fried Oreos, fried bacon-wrapped steaks, fried fried dough and every other culinary achievement. But now, his senses were attuned, and he could see and hear their message more clearly.

One of them was a trucker from the highways, bearded and grimy, baseball cap covering a pale, fleshy skull, eyes a little too bright. "I'd only been drinking a little," the trucker ghost said. "Barely anything. Maybe five beers, maybe a shot or two of whiskey. If the damn roads had been kept up better, well, shit, I wouldn't have turned over at all."

Another was the keeper of a gas station, an elderly woman with hair pulled back in a matronly bun, her eyes cross. "These damn kids, they got no respect anymore. Pulling guns on respectable business owners. They ought to be taught to *use* them right, if nothing else."

The third was a farmer from the 1920s, big beard, dirty overalls, pitchfork in hand. "I kept telling 'em I was alright. That it was just a cold and it wasn't even that bad. Doctor kept throwing around words like 'polio' and such. But pah to that! I don't need some hifalutin quack tellin' me all his liberal opinions! Ain't got the time for that."

Myron was transfixed by all this. He didn't know what to make of it. "So what?" he asked. "Do you want me to do something? Stop the carnival, or something like that?"

At this, all of them laughed together, a horrible cacophonous noise like nails on chalkboards. "God, no!" exclaimed the farmer. "Why would we want that? This carnival's the most interesting thing to happen here in *ages!*"

"No," the gas station owner said, leering at him. "If anything, we like *you* in particular. You ought to come join us! Be a part of our eternal party!"

Myron didn't know what to say. He supposed some part of him was flattered.

In his haze of thought, trying to take in the grand proposition the ghosts had given him – he'd never before felt so *wanted* – Myron drove around after work that day. He found himself intrinsically drawn to the old Victorian. Rose's house. He just needed to *see* it again, to take in the majesty at least one more time before he put her out of his head.

And he looked upon its dark, splendid glory again, and felt such a sense of beauty and purpose in the world.

For about one brief moment.

Then the car pulled up close to the house and Rose got out with a new guy, taller than Myron, conventionally attractive. Myron thought he looked like a magazine model. All wavy hair, fine skin, probably used lotions with unpronounceable names. And then a rush of jealousy filled him like fire. He hadn't even known he was capable of *that*.

Consulting with the ghosts again later, sitting on the merry go round, Myron sulked. "How could she *do* that," he wondered aloud, his hands and chin resting on the top of a porcelain painted toy horse. "How could she move on so *quickly?*"

"I always did think this country was going to hell, soon as women got the vote," the old farmer said.

"Hey, now," the gas station owner said sternly.

"Just sayin'," the farmer said, raising his hands in a gesture of surrender. "What's all this new *choice* good for? Just marry the farm girl from down the road, have a litter of kids. Life ain't got to be so complicated."

"You're out of your element, you dumb hick," the gas station owner said. "Stay in your lane."

The farmer looked crestfallen at this.

Myron didn't know what to do with the farmer's spiel. He chalked it up to a translation barrier. Different times.

The trucker said, "Maybe you ought to show her. Maybe you both come join us forever. Make her your ghost bride."

Now that, Myron thought, was an *idea*.

In the night he went to the Victorian again, feeling the fluttering inside him as he entered his beloved. He found Rose asleep in her bed, covers pulled up to her chin, and he took out the chloroform he'd purloined that day, from an unsuspecting medicine man at the town pharmacy. It had been easy to get, really.

And it was easy to slip it over Rose's mouth and nose as she woke up to the sound of his footsteps, her eyes wide, a scream forming but snuffed out.

Rose woke up in the open night air, cold in just her shorts and a tank top. She was strapped into something; a fair ride. As her brain woke up little by little, she realized it was the Fireball. Once at a county fair when she was fourteen, a friend had goaded her to go on this ride. It had spun her out and afterwards she threw up in a trash can shaped like a clown's head and said never again.

She felt groggy, too; like she'd been drugged, and her eyesight was blurred. There was movement to her left. She turned and could make out a slender figure, dark and moving frenetically... it was Myron, she realized.

"What is this shit, Myron?" she asked.

"Hell," he said, "just doin' my job. Fair inspector."

"Let me out," she said. Pushing on the bar across her torso did nothing. She had been locked in.

"You shouldn't've gone with that other asshole," Myron said.

He pushed a button on his cell phone, and they were beginning to rise. The air got colder, and the wind kicked up, harsh against her bare legs and arms.

"Let us down," she said.

"You never seemed to appreciate what I did," he said, gesturing to the fair around him. "This is a *sacred tradition*. I'm the *guardian* of all this. I'm the heart and soul. And you wanted some other guy, some random asshole, rather than me. I see how it is!"

"He's a med student, asshole!" Rose shouted.

But the gears on the ride were creaking and bending in the weight. A flame was kindling at the base of the claw-arm of the ride. It began to spread, and the smoke was rising.

"God," Rose said, and her life began to flash before her eyes. She wondered if people would remember her well. There was Ryan, asleep now and waiting to come see her later on that weekend. And her friend who'd introduced them.

At least if she died, she thought, she could pester her grandma about why she'd given her the damn house in the first place. That had been what started all this, after all. So that was a light at the end of the tunnel – well, provided there *was* something after.

Rose supposed she would find out soon.

And the claw of the fireball, with the both of them in it, spun back and forth, back and forth, and Myron's face when she looked over had the look of a demon, wide toothy mouth and evil eyes. The top of the claw hit a high point and Rose's head knocked back, the smoke filling her nostrils and then every other part of her too, and she felt a sense of *leaving*.

Then she was in the black space and felt no more pain or cold, smelled no more smoke. There were three figures approaching, footsteps echoing like on a hard tile floor. It was a farmer wielding a pitchfork, an elderly woman with a gas station nametag and a trucker with a baseball cap. They were *there* but they had a kind of ethereal, spiritual glow, bright and exuberant golden yellow, about them.

"Only you've made it over so far," the trucker said.

"What?" Rose asked. "What's happening?"

"So young," the gas station woman said, pity in her voice and eyes, her glow changing to a more sympathetic, gentle blue shade. "It seems a waste, to be here."

"The other one, the boy, was better," the farmer said.

"How about we send you back?" the woman asked.

"Back?" Rose asked.

"We send you back, for a do-over," the woman said. "You send *him* here. Him alone."

Rose's head was spinning and all she could do was nod.

Then, back in the cloud of smoke as the Fireball whirled 'round and 'round, she woke up. The pain and the cold were back. But also there was a change: her harness had been undone, and she was free to move.

Myron, beside her, had his face tilted up to the wind. His eyes widened, though, when she lunged over and put her hands around his throat. She squeezed and could feel the skin and the pulse underneath thrashing and flailing. All her life and she'd never even been in a fight. Now this. She almost wanted to laugh.

His eyes were bulging. He was trying to say something, his mouth moving, spittle forming. But no words. This was not like in the movies where the dying got to have their dramatic Last Words. Instead she just kept squeezing and the smoke kept billowing until the life was out of him.

The Fireball was dipping down towards the ground again. The fire and the smoke were now covering everything, and she felt lightheaded. There would be firefighters and questions soon, if she could even escape this now, which was a dubious prospect at best...

But, not thinking at all, she took a lunge as the ride's claw-hand was at its lowest point. Her shoulder hit the metal ground, which was hot with the fire, but she kept rolling until she was on the grass. She spat some of her own hair out of her mouth, dizzy and disoriented but very much *alive*. The cold air was striking on her skin, forming goosebumps and making her shiver, and she was grateful for that now.

And she took a deep breath as the Fireball swung its pendulum arc again, watching it burn, the fires climbing up and up, consuming it entirely.

The fire trucks were coming, like sentinels, red lights flashing. But there were also spectators now. There was a burly brown-skinned man in a chef's apron standing there agape, and an elderly couple, craggy and worn. Rose realized that, in actuality, this was to be the first day of the fair in Silver Lake.

The first day, she thought, and this happened.

What a start.

She walked to the man in the chef's apron, who regarded her with incredulity. "Holy shit," he said. "What happened here?"

Rose shook her head. "I can't even begin to explain. You're dressed like a chef. You cook stuff here?"

"I'm going to, yeah," he said, still flabbergasted.

"What're you gonna be cooking?"

"Mostly fried treats. Fried Oreos. Fried ice cream."

"Some fried Oreos could go down well, actually," she said. He looked at her quizzically, but then shrugged and began walking down the row of tents, and she followed, her stomach growling something fierce.

ABOUT THE AUTHOR

Larry Griffin is a writer from Florida, raised on a diet of horror movies, heavy metal music and crime literature. When not writing or performing stand-up comedy, he can be found at a beach or a movie theater.

TOURIST

Brandon Mead

There's a joke that whispers between the locals in Las Vegas about the bathrooms at a certain casino and hotel on The Strip. An urban legend, spread to tourists and vacationers that always starts with a giggle, then a gasp, then a shaking of the head punctuated with a serious tone and audible question, "Really?"

Parking has gotten incredibly expensive as the violence on the two most interesting miles in North America has waxed and waned. The Mojave Desert was colonized by an unlikely coupling of the American Mafia and Mormon Church that built towers full of money surrounded by low-income housing to support it. Some of the complexes are still named after the gangsters, but none of the religious figures. It's the kind of theme park history no one wants to talk about.

Even if he's not staying there, a Tourist could park in the garages of the combination hotel/casinos. Spend the Disney prices to be close to the action. But regardless of how things look in that Zach Galifianakis movie, don't underestimate the distance between anything tall and erect. If the lonely Tourist on vacation with his family hears the urban legend while he's at the casino with the replica of the Statue of David and gets curious, it will take him at least two hours to walk his flip-flops to the setting of the rumor.

Some Usher at a show with a vest on may tell the man at low volume to look for red and white stripes. He could mention to go up the first escalator, then take a right. He probably cupped over one side of his mouth when told the Tourist, "Crooked door. Middle stall. The one with the holes in both sides."

The Strip, cannot be expanded further north. Every piece of land that exists in the upper-most stretch is the only space available. If some mogul comes along with a bright idea to add to the entertainment capital of the world, the hotels on the north-side either keep building up to the sky or tear something down to start over. Almost every inch has become some sort of burial ground for whatever was hot the decade before. A neon-lit cemetery for showgirls, lounge singers, and Elvis impersonators.

Toes dirty from the mix of constant demolition and reconstruction, this Tourist is already counting how many hours he may have before his wife and kids wake-up in their hotel room. Whether he could sneak a ride-share back onto the joint credit card instead of walk-of-shaming back through the two hours of buzzing lights and intoxicating commotion. The programmed dings of slot machines and interactive LED billboards. Plastic tubes full of bright tangerine Slushee liquor so long people need a strap around their neck to hold them. Maybe he could navigate it all back in the safety of a stranger's car, if he made it back at all.

His new adventure wasn't the same as opening an app on his phone in his little southern town. Turning himself into an unnamed torso or shady face in a bathhouse. This was the holy grail of anonymous hook-ups. This, he reassured himself again finally nearing the doors with the giant plaster clown statue looming overhead, was going to be the best head of his life.

This place, it's been around just as long as Bugsy Siegel's been dead in the desert. It got famous for running aerial trapeze acts above the slot machines and still runs shows twelve hours a day, every hour on the hour, of different circus routines. The way you feel when you walk inside is the same way you feel at any carnival. A little excited, a little filthy; like you want to smile, but also keep checking on your wallet. Make sure some all-teeth clown or cute tightrope walker wasn't being friendly enough to slip it out of your back pocket.

Because as much as this place wants to be known as the most family-friendly building on The Strip, there's a reason it offers the lowest price for rooms. There's a reason you can get the same quote for two queen beds as you could in the seventies. Because, unlike all the sky-high construction of the south-side, nothing on the north-side has changed. The ghosts of Las Vegas live where distorted carnival music still plays twenty-four hours a day.

Tourist by Brandon Mead

A Dealer at a place named after a single tall pink bird will tell the Tourist, it's just as likely one of those Mormon fellows as it is one of the Mobsters. This guy, his cuffs are pushed up to his elbows and tied off with something that clasps shut. It's part of the uniform, to show he's got nothing to hide. He's been shuffling cards in thick cigarette smoke for almost four decades and in his gravelly voice, tells the kind of men that sneak out of their hotel rooms after 2 a.m., "Does it matter? Whatever it is in there could suck the paint off a skyscraper."

So the Tourist goes to the place marketed with the most smiles. The one that's a constant joke because of how it looks when the man gets inside. Old and falling apart. Rainbow carpet rolling back with black mold and brown mildew. Everything reeking with clown make-up and cheap cigar smoke.

And this closeted Tourist, Clark Griswalding his own blonde in the red convertible, trolling the The Strip for ghost dick; he sees the red and white stripes, then the escalator. The entire ride up, mirrors on either side reflecting what he can't just leave in Vegas. What he's always trying to forget in Tallahassee or Birmingham.

He takes a right and finds the men's room with the crooked door. There's only three stalls when he gets inside, the scent changing from smoke to crystallized urine. The kind of locker room stench of testosterone and dry sweat. The right hormone and chemical combination to get the Tourist aroused by his own bad decisions while he closes the middle stall door behind him and latches it shut. Thick as the pyramid on the south-side and longer than the light shooting from the top that can be seen from space, he pushes through the jagged edges of the pressed wood stall divider. The aged cork soaking wet from whoever followed the cryptic directions before him. Everything sticky and crumbling under the weight of paranormal saliva. Some spirit that just can't let go of making sure every Tourist enjoys his stay in Sin City. That they love the thing he built for them. This place, where they can do anything.

Something grabs hold with skilled hands from the left side, and it's glorious, heavenly. The Tourist, he doesn't want to end his adventure too soon, and switches to the other damp hole on the right side. A well-trained mouth responds, offering otherworldly head. Hard and soft palettes of satin, a tongue and lips made for just this purpose. Moans at low tones echoing from the striped and peeling bathroom wallpaper, he switches back to the left side of the stall, the expert palms and fingers.

DEMONIC CARNIVAL

A perfect grip and stroke with exactly the right amount of pressure and release. Mustaches, stubble, and hairy knuckles tickling the more sensitive skin of the Tourist's body. The things he couldn't have on a regular basis in Charleston or Greensboro.

It's when everything is done, going back and forth between the left and ride sides, over and over again, till he's spent and head-back, leaning and sighing against a toilet clogged with paper towels and cigarette butts; that he gets curious. The Tourist has to know what apparitions were responsible for such an intense sexual encounter. He bends down slowly to look through the moist openings, looking right and then left. Expecting to see something ghostly or ghastly, some guts or bones that would make him regret his funhouse adventure. But through the hole on the right, he sees just the shoulder of a vest. And through the left, a band holding up a cuffed sleeve.

From either side of the stalls comes laughter, less chilling than the Tourist was expecting when he had anticipated the unearthed remains of some missionary or mob errand boy with a slight lisp. Something grosser than the way his flip-flops stuck to the floor of the casino carnival bathroom.

The Usher on the right, he's wiping around the corners of his mouth when he whispers through the rough hole to the Tourist, "Glad you found the place."

The Dealer is lighting a cigarette when he adds, "I'll give you a ride back to your family."

The Usher is almost laughing when he says, "What happens in Vegas..?"

He lets his remark trail off, no need to finish the question. No reason to wait longer for what would either end in a direct punch coming through the glory hole or an echoed line from a marketing campaign Vegas would never fully recover from.

And the Tourist, he doesn't say anything right away. Surrounded by Mormons and Mobsters, the death and rebirth of entertainment, the constant cycle of letting people believe they can be anything they want to be within the city limits; the promise of being their worst self to discover their best self—the Tourist thinks for a minute, slowly pulling-up the soles of his shoes from the tacky multi-colored tile and soiled grout. Wondering if he'd ever learn as much about himself as he had in one night here, when he went back to Biloxi or Chattanooga, or wherever he was from.

Tourist by Brandon Mead

Saying to the Usher and the Dealer with a giggle, then a sigh, then a shaking of his head punctuated with a serious tone and audible question, "Think you could carve out one more of them there glory holes?"

ABOUT THE AUTHOR

Brandon Mead is a storyteller, cat dad, and sugar cub in the coffee shop with a composition notebook and a glitter pen. He currently resides in Las Vegas, Nevada where he is living his Nomi Malone fantasy. To read more from Brandon visit fiercestorytelling.com or follow his adventures on Instagram @FierceStorytelling

DISCOVER MORE DEMONIC ANTHOLOGIES ON AMAZON

Demonic Wildlife VOL I

You are about to set foot on a bizarre adventure, a funny fantastical one filled with demonic animals. The first few stories are light, more about the giggles, but be warned. As you read further, the dark creepy side will sneak up on you. Within this entertaining tome you will find spiders, snakes, sheep, wolves, manatees, hummingbirds, squirrels, and many more!

Demonic Household VOL II

You are traveling into a dark and humorous place. We start you off with light, soft stories, but be warned. You will find yourself falling into the ever darker, gorier, and more demonic stories with each passing page. You may look at your couch, your washer, and even television and wonder if you should be laughing anymore. Will your household turn on you? Keep your Owner's Manuals close by!

Follow us on Facebook at:

www.facebook.com/DemonicAnthologies/

https://www.facebook.com/BattleGoddessPro/

MORE BOOKS FROM 4 HORSEMEN PUBLICATIONS

ANTHOLOGIES & COLLECTIONS

4HP ANTHOLOGIES
Teen Angst: Mix Vol. 1
Teen Angst: Mix Vol. 2
My Wedding Date
The Offices of
Supernatural Being
The Sentient Space

DEMONIC ANTHOLOGIES
Demonic Wildlife
Demonic Household
Demonic Carnival
Demonic Classics
Demonic Vacations
Demonic Medicine
Demonic Workplace
& more to follow!

XXX- HOLIDAY COLLECTION
Unwrap Me
Stuffing My Stocking
Put a Little Irish in Me

FANTASY, SciFi, & PARANORMAL ROMANCE

BEAU LAKE
The Beast Beside Me
The Beast Within Me
Taming the Beast: Novella
The Beast After Me
Charming the Beast: Novella
The Beast Like Me
An Eye for Emeralds
Swimming in Sapphires
Pining for Pearls

DANIELLE ORSINO
Locked Out of Heaven
Thine Eyes of Mercy
From the Ashes
Kingdom Come
Fire, Ice, Acid, & Heart

J.M. PAQUETTE
Klauden's Ring
Solyn's Body
The Inbetween
Hannah's Heart
Call Me Forth
Invite Me In
Keep Me Close

LYRA R. SAENZ
Prelude
Falsetto in the
Woods: Novella
Ragtime Swing
Sonata
Song of the Sea
The Devil's Trill
Bercuese
To Heal a Songbird
Ghost March
Nocturne

T.S. SIMONS
Antipodes
The Liminal Space
Ouroboros
Caim
Sessrúmnir

VALERIE WILLIS
Cedric: The Demonic Knight
Romasanta: Father of
Werewolves
The Oracle: Keeper of the
Gaea's Gate
Artemis: Eye of Gaea
King Incubus: A New Reign

V.C. WILLIS
The Prince's Priest
The Priest's Assassin
The Assassin's Saint

CRIME, DETECTIVE, AND NOIR

JOE DAVISON
Journey to Hell

MARK ATLEY
Too Late to Say Goodbye
Trouble Weighs a Ton

HORROR, THRILLER, & SUSPENSE

ALAN BERKSHIRE
Jungle

AMANDA BYRD
Trapped
Moratorium
Medicate

ERIKA LANCE
Jimmy
Illusions of Happiness
No Place for Happiness
I Hunt You

MARIA DEVIVO
Witch of the Black Circle
Witch of the Red Thorn

MARK TARRANT
The Mighty Hook
The Death Riders
Howl of the Windigo
Guts and Garter Belts

FANTASY & SCIFI

**BRANDON HILL &
TERENCE PEGASUS**
Between the Devil
and the Dark

C.K. WESTBROOK
The Shooting
The Collision

D. LAMBERT
To Walk into the Sands
Rydan
Celebrant
Northlander
Esparan
King
Traitor
His Last Name

TY CARLSON
The Bench
The Favorite

DISCOVER MORE AT 4HORSEMENPUBLICATIONS.COM

www.ingramcontent.com/pod-product-compliance
Lightning Source LLC
Chambersburg PA
CBHW050333110726
47899CB00007B/2484